Unglued

Holding On: Book Two

RACHAEL BROWNELL

Unglued ~ book 2 in the Holding On series
Copyright © 2014 by Rachael Brownell.
All rights reserved.
Cover Design by Marisa Shor of Cover Me, Darling
Interior Formatting by Cassy Roop of Pink Ink Designs

PINK INK
D E S I G N S

No part of this publication may be reproduced, stored in a retrieval system or transmitted in any way by any means, electronic, mechanical, photocopy, recording, or otherwise without the prior permission of the author as provided by USA copyright law.

This novel is a work of fiction. Names, descriptions, entities, and incidents included in the story are products of the author's imagination. Any resemblance to actual persons, events, and entities is entirely coincidental.

Published in the United State of America.
ISBN: 978-149939102

For my family and friends.
Your support has meant the world to me.

Acknowledgements

There are more than a few people who have made this book a reality. Most importantly, my family and friends who have supported me through the very challenging process of getting my books published and becoming an author. I cannot thank all of you enough. Your support means the world to me.

Ardy, my sister-in-law, who read the book before I submitted it. Thank you for taking the time out of your incredibly busy life to give me some feedback. I'm sorry that I made you cry. (Twice!)

To all the bloggers and my fellow authors…there are no words to describe just how thankful I am for all the support that so many of you have shown me. It is a true blessing to be a part of a community full of such wonderful and talented people. Thank you from the bottom of my heart.

Casey Bond—you have become such an important part of all of this for me. It's the greatest feeling, knowing that there is someone I can talk to that completely understands what I am going through and who will take the time to listen to me rant. We are going to have to meet someday, because I feel like you and I will be great friends for a long time to come.

Most importantly, I want to thank the readers. Without you, there wouldn't have been a second book in the series. I hope you enjoy reading the book as much as I enjoyed writing it for all of you. Becca and Ethan's story has just begun, and I hope to eventually share with all of you their happily ever after. Thank you for taking a chance on me.

Prologue

July 2012

I was staring in the mirror when I heard him walk in. I was expecting my mom, but I was not expecting him. I was about to turn around when his scent surrounded me completely, and my body froze up. I tried to play it off like I hadn't heard him enter by adjusting my dress in the mirror one more time. My body starts to react to his the closer he gets to me, and for a brief moment, I think that I might faint. I close my eyes and hope that when I have the strength to open them again, that he will have been an illusion.

He wasn't supposed to be here. Last I knew he was in England. I'm well aware that my mom and some of our friends still speak with him on a regular basis. I would hope that if anyone knew he was coming home that they would mention it to me. Common courtesy. Common decency.

My mom was supposed to take my side after everything that happened. She, however, remained neutral, which naturally caused some friction between us that we finally have moved past. Our friends, well, I expected most of them to remain neutral, and most of them did, or at least they never mentioned it. It would have been wrong of me to ask them to choose a side. There was no point anyway. I was here and he was there. I didn't have to worry about running into him at parties or anything like that.

He's standing right behind me now, and as much as I want to

continue to ignore him, I can feel him staring at me in the mirror. I haven't opened my eyes yet because I know that if I do, I will be unable to avoid making eye contact. I don't know if I will be able to survive making eye contact with him.

We didn't part on the greatest of terms, and I haven't spoken to him since. It's been over six months, 197 days to be exact, but the pain has only begun to dull. Normally, I have enough strength to ignore it, but today, I am feeling everything. My emotions are already running the spectrum, and his presence is causing them to run even faster. I can't decide if I'm scared to open my eyes or angry because he's here.

I take a few deep breaths, and just as I'm about to open my eyes, I feel his hands on my hips, and my eyes shoot open. He's staring at me, I'm staring at him, and although there are no words between us, a lot is being said in those first few moments.

I can see his eyes darken with lust as he pulls my body closer to his. He's intertwined our fingers across my stomach, and I can feel his pulse racing under my thumb. I also see the love that he still carries with him. He's not trying to hide it.

I wonder if he can see the love that I still have for him. I wonder if he can feel it. I feel everything right now. I feel sad and happy and confused and scared. I wonder if he can see all that. I hope not. I hope he sees nothing when he looks in my eyes. My biggest fear is that he'll be able to break right through the carefully constructed walls that I've erected around my heart. I'm afraid that if he breaks through them that I will get hurt again, that I'll hurt him again.

We have yet to break eye contact, and the longer I allow him to hold me, the weaker my knees are going to get. For every ounce of fear I'm holding on to right now, I'm also holding on to twice as much love. I feel like a puddle of mush on the inside. My heart is racing, and my stomach feels like there are about a million butterflies trying to escape.

I have dreamt about this moment for so long. I've wanted him to hold me like he used to. I've wanted to feel his strong arms wrap around me, his breath on my neck as he kisses that sweet spot behind my ear that I love so much. I never thought this day would come, and now that it's here, I don't know how to react.

My body is telling me one thing, and my mind is telling me another. I have to stop this. I have to get out of this embrace before someone else comes in the room. I have to pull away before I am never able to break free of him. My brain is allowing the pain to break free, and all I can think about is how he left me.

My mind is telling my body all these things, but my body decides to betray my mind. Instead of pulling away, I sink further into his arms. I rest my head back against his chest, and he tightens his told on me. I want to nuzzle into his neck. I want to pull his face down and kiss him. I want to get out of this dress and run away…

That's when my brain finally takes full control and I pull away. He ran away from me. He left me. He broke off our engagement. I may not have been perfect, actually I was far from it, but I admitted my mistakes. He was supposed to forgive me. He was supposed to love me unconditionally. He was supposed to be my best friend, my soul mate, "the one."

It took me months of crying and beating myself up to finally move on in my life. He has no right barging in here—today, of all days—and decide to forgive me now. I forgave myself a while ago, and I don't need his forgiveness anymore. I am with someone who wants to be with me, broken pieces of my heart and all. He is not allowed to do this to me.

"I can't do this. Not today, and not any time soon."

I tried to sound as sure and as bold as I could muster. I was not going to allow myself to cry, especially not in front of him. I would consider them wasted tears. I wasted tears on him for months before I realized that I needed to move on. I may always love him, but I would not shed another tear because of him.

"I'm sorry. I'm sorry for…everything. I know—"

"Stop. I really can't hear this right now. You shouldn't be here. You are supposed to be on another continent right now, not standing next to me in my room."

I know that the way I said it must have made a statement because he actually took two steps back. I wasn't yelling. I wasn't even trying to sound mean at this point, although I'm sure that I did a little. I was just trying to get my point across, and I think that I made myself perfectly clear.

"I came back this morning. I needed…wanted to be here today, for you. I wanted to make sure that you are all right. I've always tried to be there for you."

"Except when I really needed you to be! Except when I needed you to forgive me, so that we could move on with our life *together*!"

Unglued

Now I'm screaming. I know that the right thing to do is to have this conversation. It's long overdue, and it would put an end to everything that I have been internalizing since he left. Yes. I need to have this conversation with him, but there was no way I was going to be able to just talk with him right now. Right now, all I want to do is yell, because the anger that's been building has taken over.

"I needed you then. I have needed you for the past six months. I needed you to be the person I fell in love with when I told you how I felt, when I told you what happened."

I can see the sorrow on his face. I can see the fact that I've hurt him with my words. At that moment, I really didn't care. I needed to get to the church. I needed to get out of that room and find the strength to move on with my life, because at that moment I was questioning everything, and I didn't like the way it was making me feel.

I grabbed my purse off my bed and stormed past him. My mom is sitting at the bar in the kitchen waiting for me with a tentative smile. When I don't return her smile, she picks up her purse and follows me out the door. My car is blocked in by his, maybe his way of preventing me from leaving, but my mom's is parked on the street. I jumped in the car and waited patiently for her to catch up to me.

The drive to the church is quiet. My heart hasn't stopped racing since he walked into my room, I'm not sure if it ever will, and it's all I can hear, all I can feel. I can feel it breaking more and more the closer we get to the church. The combination of what just happened and what's about to happen is going to cause it to shatter completely.

I need air, fresh air. It's over one hundred degrees today so I dare not roll down the window and let the AC out. I feel like I'm going to hyperventilate. My breathing has become erratic, and I can't stop shaking. My heart is pounding in my chest, and it feels like it might break out. I'm starting to sweat, and just as a bead trickles down the back of my neck, I bend forward and puked up my breakfast. I barely miss my shoes and my dress somehow.

Without saying anything at all, I felt my mom pull the car over. I heard her get out, and the next thing I know, my door is opening. I can feel her unbuckling my seatbelt and pulling me out, but I'm not really there. I stand against the side of the car and just stared off into space. I'm not sure what I was looking at, or where we were, but a moment later, I was being ushered back into the now puke-free car and handed a bottle of water.

As we pulled up to the church, I popped a couple mints and stepped out of the car. I smoothed out my dress and held my head high as I walked in the side door to where I knew friends and family were waiting. I felt nothing at that moment. My emotions were stowed deep down, and I was going to do everything I could to keep them there today. Nothing was going to unnerve them. I was going to be strong. I've been putting on a show for everyone for so long now, I was sure no one would notice. Fake smile, check.

We visited for a short amount of time before the pastor came to summon everyone. I quickly pulled my veil down and found my mom. As we walked up the center aisle, I feel those emotions begin to creep up and try to overwhelm me again. I held my head a little higher and looked straight ahead and found him, my rock. His face was warm and welcoming and calmed me just a little.

"Why, Mom?" I whisper. "Why did you call him and ask him to come?"

"I didn't, I swear. I haven't spoken to him in almost two months. He stopped calling when I told him that I thought you had moved on. I was just as surprised as you when he showed up today."

"If it wasn't you, then who was it?"

"I don't know, Becca, but does it really matter right now?"

I knew she was right. It didn't matter today, and it probably wouldn't matter tomorrow. Whoever called him had every right. It wasn't my place to keep him away from his home. He was free to visit whenever he wanted to. Today, of all days, was no exception. Was he here right now, though? I want to turn around and find out, but I don't. I need to focus and the only way I am going to be able to do that is to keep my eyes lock on his.

Everything is going to be just fine. I keep repeating that to myself the rest of the way to the front of the church, and by the time we reach the end of the aisle, I almost believe it. If I hadn't broken eye contact and looked down at my dead friend, I would have fallen for my own lie. It's at that moment that I come completely unglued.

Crap!

Chapter One

December 2011

Just staring at the mess that was in front of me was starting to freak me out a little. My planner is highlighted every color of the rainbow with a dozen dates circled. This was gonna be a crazy month, and I didn't even know where to begin.

My birthday is tomorrow, and I needed to clean the house for the guests that we were having over. Brad's birthday is next week. I have finals to study for at some point during all of the celebrating, and Ethan is graduating in two weeks. The overachiever that he has become is graduating after only three and a half years of college, instead of four like most normal people.

After that comes the holidays, and this year is our year to host the New Year's Eve party. I was going to need to take January off just to catch myself back up on sleep. Of course, that's not possible, so I am just gonna have to make the best of things as usual.

One thing at a time. First, I need to clean this house: kitchen, main floor bathroom, living room, and the back patio. Let's not forget the growing pile of dirty clothes on the floor of our bedroom. I love Ethan to death, but he is not really great at picking up after himself.

All those years, his parents paid someone else to clean and do laundry; they never really taught him to take care of himself. Without me following behind him, picking up the clothes he tosses everywhere, loading the dishwasher, putting the toilet seat down, he would be living in a sea of dirty everything.

Laundry. Okay, let's separate the whites and darks and get this show on the road. I grab my iPod, hit the shuffle button on some new music that I just downloaded, and crank the volume just high enough to drown out everything around me. Tackling the house, the cleaning, the laundry, exams, and my life seems to be just a little easier when I have some good music to drown out all the static that tends to surround me.

I get the whites in the washer, and headed back to get a load of towels and sheets to go in next. I stripped our bed and the guest bed, throwing the dirty sheets into the hallway to create a new pile. I stared at the naked bed knowing what has to come next, and I can feel the dread starting to brew inside of me. I slowly backed out of the room and walked the ten feet down the hall to the linen closet. I opened it up and stared at the sheets that are sitting on the shelf that is just above my shoulder.

This should be an easy task: grab the sheets, and head back to the room to make the bed. For me, this is the hardest part of cleaning the house. I always get it out of the way first so that I can take out my frustration on the rest of the house, scrubbing and cleaning, but it never really gets any easier. It never makes me stronger. It never takes away the dread of this moment.

I've thought about putting the sheets on a lower shelf just to avoid the anger that begins to well up inside of me, but I would consider that cheating. I will always tackle anything that's thrown my way head on, I promised myself that last spring. I will not run from a challenge, and I will not back down. This is my life, and I will not let this one thing define who I am.

Who was I kidding? I wanted to cheat, and reach up with my left hand, and pull the sheets down, and I almost do, but I stop myself. I need to do this because I need to prove to myself that it gets easier every time. It may not feel like it gets easier but it does, it has to, it will eventually. So I reached up with my right hand, and just as I'm about to get to the sheets, I feel a bolt of pain run straight from my hand to my shoulder, and I instinctively pulled my hand back down. I will get these damn sheets if it takes me all day.

I have to walk away. Getting all worked up and angry doesn't do me any good. I headed back to the guest room, and grabbed the vacuum out of the closet. This I can do without fearing pain, without fearing my inability to complete a simple task. This I have mastered over the last seven months so that I don't feel the pain. So I vacuumed the entire upstairs, dreading the painful moment that I will have to return to the linen closet and pull down those sheets. I should just use my left hand and get it over with.

By the time the entire upstairs was cleaned, bathroom and all, I can almost hear the linen closet calling my name. I spend what feels like forever staring at those sheets again, and know that I need to keep moving and finish cleaning the house. I have a ton of things still to accomplish, and I can't let this get the best of me. I am stronger than that.

Reaching up, I can feel my muscles start to tighten as my arm stretches above my head. I pulled my arm back down and go through some of the exercises my therapist still has me doing. Once I felt the muscles start to loosen, I reached up again, but my arm doesn't seem to want to stretch the way I want it to, so I repeat the stretches again. I will get those damn sheets if it's the last thing I do today!

I finally gave in and reached up quickly, standing on the tips of my toes to give me just a few less inches to stretch, and snagged the sheets before my arm completely feels like it's on fire from the pain. They drop out of my grasp and onto the floor, but I've gotten them off the shelf. It's a small accomplishment but I feel great, except the burning sensation that's still lingering.

Two hours later, the house is completely clean, and the last load of laundry is in the dryer. My goal for the day has been accomplished. I'm putting all the folded towels and sheets in the linen closet when I feel his presence behind me. My body has been tuned in to his for years, so even though I didn't hear him come in, I know he's here. I still jump when he slides his hands around my waste, but not as high as I used to. I let him hold me for just a few minutes before I pull out my ear buds.

"Hey."

"Hey yourself, gorgeous."

"How was work today?"

"Not bad, actually." He hates his job and we both know it. Any day that he comes home and says *not bad* is a good day at work for him. "The house looks great. Need any help finishing up?"

He knows that I have trouble putting the clean sheets away. I normally let him help me or leave them out, indicating that I couldn't do it, but today I need to conquer this. I've spent seven month avoiding the things that I can't do, and with the New Year coming around, I plan on conquering all my fears.

"No thanks. I just need to put these sheets away and wait for the last load to dry. I started dinner. It should be done in a few minutes if you want to change and set the table." I can feel the smile on his face as he kisses that spot on my neck that drives me crazy. I know he's proud of how far I've come since my injury. I just don't know if I can be proud of myself yet.

"All right. I'll see you down there in a few minutes then?"

"Yep."

"What do you want to drink?"

"White wine if we have any."

"Okay. I love you."

"I love you too."

With that, he's gone. I know he's just around the corner in our bedroom, but I still feel like he can see me, so I wait. Once I hear him begin to descend the stairs, I pick up the folded sheets from the basket and stare at the shelf that they go on. I can do this. I just have to reach up and slide them on the shelf. It's barely a reach to be honest with you. The shelf is only about an inch above my head. I can reach it. I just need to be able to reach it without causing myself pain.

∞

This day was not going how I planned. I woke up to find that my best racquet popped a string. I was going to need to use my backup, and I hadn't played with it in months. The tension in the strings needed to be adjusted, but I was going to have to make it work.

Ethan wasn't going to be able to make it to my match on account of his uber-bitchy boss. I really wished he would find a new job.

Then, five minutes ago, I find out that I'm playing my least favorite person, my archrival. She's not a great player, but she's gotten better over the years. The big problem with her is that she likes to play dirty sometimes because she hasn't been able to beat me yet. Our rivalry has only gotten stronger over the years, and as much as I dislike her as a person, I have grown to hate playing against her because of her nasty attitude.

So not how I expected my day to start. I'll deal with it, of course. I always make the best of a crappy day, and lately, I have been coming out on top. I've only lost once this season, and that's a whole lot better than my first season.

My first year with the team was pretty crazy. I played well but was completely unprepared for how well everyone else was going to be playing. I thought that playing on the "Super Seniors" team would have given me an advantage but it didn't. I lost about 40 percent of my matches, and now I have something to prove.

I have to play my best this season or I may lose my scholarship. They haven't said as much to me, but I can feel it when they watch me. I feel like I'm under a microscope most of the time, and right now it's helping me to focus more and play better tennis. It's a double-edged sword, but it's motivating me so I can't really complain.

Crap!

They changed my match time. I see my opponent is already on the court waiting for me. The official is staring at his watch which means I'm late. I started to jog over to the court. I toss my bag just outside of the gate after grabbing my racquet and I quickly popped down on the court and started to stretch when the judge begins to walk my way.

"I'm sorry, but we need to start right now. You are officially fifteen minutes late, and had you not just walked through that gate, you would have forfeited your match."

Wow! Really? I can see her snickering behind the official, but I don't let her get to me. I popped up off the court and stretched my arms as I walked to the net to shake her hand. She's already sweaty which tells me that she took advantage of my tardiness and got in some practice. I, however, have cold muscles. That's not a good thing when it comes to tennis. You need to make sure that your muscles are loose. Hopefully, my muscles warm up quickly.

That didn't happen. Her first serve was out, and her second was just out of my reach. I dove, missed the ball with my racquet, and landed *hard* on my right shoulder, and hit my head on the court. That's the last thing I remembered from that day.

I woke up two days later in the hospital with my entire arm immobilized, casted from the shoulder down. My greatest fear was quickly becoming a reality. I was injured, again. Not only that, I injured the same shoulder I had in high school. It didn't take a genius to figure out that I may be looking at the end of my playing days.

The way I landed popped my shoulder in the opposite direction I had before, dislocating it, and causing a portion of my collarbone to chip away. I had undergone surgery while I was unconscious to repair the break, but the doctor said that my shoulder was never going to be the same again. "Limited mobility" were the exact words he used. No one had to tell me these facts, I already knew the outcome.

I spent two more days in the hospital under observation for a possible concussion. Once I was released, I locked myself in the house and refused visitors. I sat in bed and cried all day. My phone was constantly vibrating with calls from teammates and texts from friends. I didn't return a single one of them. I was depressed, and I didn't want anyone to know.

Ethan was great during my "tantrum" following the accident. He allowed me to cry when I needed to, and held me when I would let him. He brought home my homework from all my classes and spoke to the teachers about what happened, even though most of them knew since there was a front page picture of me unconscious on the court in the school paper. He even respected my decision to turn away all visitors in the beginning, but I knew that wouldn't last for long.

The hardest part was showering. I took a bath most days since it was easier to keep my cast out of the water, but it was a challenge to wash my hair in the tub. After a week of Ethan helping me bathe and washing my hair, I was over it. I wanted a shower in the worst way. I knew that I was going to need his help still, so as he slipped in one morning, I covered my cast the best I could in a garbage bag and slipped in with him.

That may have been the single best shower of my life. My hair felt fresh and clean, and my confidence may have been a little bit renewed. It's amazing what a week of frustration and depression and abstinence can do to a horny young woman. Put her in the right situation and all her troubles will melt away. I know mine felt like they did. I started to feel like myself again as I stepped out of the shower. Stepping into the kitchen in just my robe that morning was a whole other story.

"What are you doing here?" I tightened the strap on my robe the best I could and held it together with my left hand.

"I know you don't want visitors, but I was pretty sure that didn't include me."

"Um, that includes everyone when I am wearing just my robe."

His smile made my stomach tighten a little, and the way he was looking at me was not a good thing. If Ethan weren't upstairs, I would be afraid to make a move, any move. I would be afraid he would pounce on me. He's been looking at me this way for too long now and it needs to stop. He knows it and I know it.

"I'm gonna go get dressed. Help yourself to coffee if you want some. Ethan should be down in a minute." That's all it took to wipe the smile off of his face, the mention of Ethan, and there was his "friend face." Before things could get weird again, I slipped out of the kitchen and upstairs to get changed.

Reach up, just a little higher. I can do this. Almost there. Just a little… Crap! My entire arm is engulfed in pain. It feels like it's on fire, and my muscles are starting to cramp up. The sheets have dropped to the floor, and I drop beside them. I can feel the tears streaming down my face, but I'm not sure if I'm crying because of the pain or because of my failure. Either way, the sheets are still in a pile on the floor.

Chapter Two

After the breakdown I had last night, the last thing I wanted to do was celebrate my birthday. Turning twenty-one was supposed to be exciting, but I wasn't really that excited. I didn't feel like I had too much to celebrate this year. Don't get me wrong, I had plenty going on for me: good grades, a great boyfriend of over three and a half years, loving friends and family. The list could literally go on and on. The one thing I didn't have right now was the one thing that I wanted most. I wanted to be able to play tennis again.

The New Year is approaching. I had to keep reminding myself that I was going to conquer all my fears next year. I was going to pick up my racquet again. I was going to hit a ball. I may never play as well as I used to play, but I was not going to let anyone tell me that I was not able to try. I was definitely going to try.

With our friends' arrival approaching, I take one last look at the linen closet with disgust. Ethan left the sheets on the floor because I asked him to. I wanted to be able to take care of them myself, and if it wasn't going to happen yesterday, then it was going to happen right now. I slowly made my approach, like I was sneaking up on a sleeping bear. I was scared that I wouldn't be able to do it. When I heard the front door open and footsteps on the stairs, I knew that it was now or never.

Get it over with.
You can do this! You can do this!

Unglued

I kept repeating that in my head the entire time I picked up the sheets, lifted them above my head, and as I was about the slip them on the shelf, I caught movement out of the corner of my eye. I turned my head, and that was all it took to slip them on the shelf. I didn't even realize that I had put them up there until Ethan started to smile at me.

I smiled back at him until I realized that the sheets were back on the shelf. My smile turned to pure shock when I realized that my shoulder wasn't on fire with pain. Before I knew what was happening, I was jumping into his arms with nothing but pure joy and excitement in my heart. It was a small feat, but it felt like I moved a mountain.

"I did it." I'm not sure why I was whispering but I was.

"I know. I saw the whole thing."

"I don't understand." I pulled out of his embrace and just stared at the linen closet. "Did you move the shelf down?"

"No. I don't think those shelves move. I'm pretty sure you did that all by yourself."

"Well, I think that calls for a drink." I turned around and my smile matched his. "Wanna come celebrate with me?"

Hand in hand, we walked to the kitchen to pour ourselves a drink, my first official, legal, drink. White wine had become a favorite over the past couple of months. After being on pain medication for two months, my "tolerance" for liquor was gone, and as much as I like beer, it's never been a favorite of mine. When my cast came off and we celebrated, Ethan brought home a bottle of white wine and I've been in love ever since.

Ethan turned up the music and I pulled out the snacks. I was one of the first of my friends to turn twenty-one, so I knew that some of them would be sleeping on my floor tonight. I had already started trading booze for keys and hiding them in a cupboard. More people started to arrive and our living room suddenly felt a bit crowded. I opened the sliding door to the backyard and, like magic, people started to migrate out. It was December, but in Tucson, that meant forty degrees at night.

I went to grab a handful of chips, but as I was reaching in the bowl, I realized that I hadn't put any jewelry on. I grabbed my wine and quickly went back up the stairs to our room. I could see my jewelry tray resting on the top of my dresser as I approached. My emerald ring sparkling in the light, shining in from our window.

I hadn't worn it since Ethan and I moved in together, just the two of us. It seemed almost wrong in a way. I wanted Ethan to know that my heart belonged to him, and that whatever I had with Brad, that I was no longer holding on to it. He was my future.

I fingered the ring for just a few minutes before I heard him enter the room. He cleared his throat just about the time his scent reached me. There are only two people in this world that I would be able to identify by scent alone. Ethan—who was probably downstairs entertaining our guests that were starting to arrive—was one, and Brad was the other.

"So, are you gonna put it on? I haven't seen you wear it in a while, and if I remember correctly, you told me once that you would never take it off. Or were you just telling me that because I was laid up in a hospital bed on the verge of dying?"

I could help but let out a little laugh. He was so dramatic sometimes.

"First off, you were not even close to dying. Secondly, I don't remember actually using the word promise. And lastly, I do still wear it from time to time, but it reminds me of my past, and right now, I need to focus on moving forward with my life. So, no, I don't plan on wearing it today, but that doesn't mean that I still don't appreciate its beauty from time to time."

I set the ring back down on the tray, and picked up my emerald earrings and a matching bracelet that Ethan had gotten me last year for Christmas. I never turned around to face him, but I could tell that his demeanor had changed. The room was no longer filled with energy but with uncertainty. This is not how I wanted my party to start. I had to apologize. I didn't mean to hurt his feelings, but it had to be said. I hated that I had to constantly remind him that I was with Ethan, especially after all this time.

When I finally had the nerve to turn around, he was gone. When I say gone, I literally mean gone. His scent was the only thing that remained. He wasn't downstairs when I got down there and no one had seen him. No one had even noticed him arrive earlier. It's like he was never even here, except the present I found on my dresser later that night.

After getting the cast off, I thought my life would go back to normal. I was wrong, on so many levels. I missed tennis more than I

Unglued

imagined I ever could, and not being able to do a lot of things for myself right away, made me dependent on everyone around me. I think that's what bothered me the most. The fact that I felt incapable of taking care of myself. Ethan understood my frustration most of the time and we were able to work through it, but things started to get tense between us anyway.

My emotions were all over the map, and if I wasn't crying, I was most likely angry about something. I blamed my injury on my coach for not telling me my match time had changed. I blamed the official for not allowing me to stretch. Mostly, I blamed myself for going after a shot that I should have let go. My ego was the root cause of the injury, but I couldn't bring myself to blame myself. I wanted to point the finger elsewhere so that I had someone to focus my anger on.

Three months of therapy. I had gone through it before and survived, and I assumed I would survive again. This injury was different though. I was having trouble with the smallest tasks, and if I turned my shoulder just right, I would get shooting pains. After the first week of driving myself to therapy, I had to start relying on others to help me. I could get myself there just fine, but the drive home was painful. Anytime I had to steer the car or turn left, I would almost break out in tears. The movement was just too much for my shoulder after an hour of physical therapy.

Brad was my go-to guy for this. His class schedule was similar to mine, so he had the same mornings off that I did. He would come and pick me up, we would go for coffee, and then he would take me to therapy. His topics of conversation were always light on the way there, trying to keep things positive, and helped me to focus on anything other than where we were headed. On the way back, my anger would kick in, and if we talked at all, he would take my verbal beating without a defensive word.

We grew close again by the end of the three months. It felt like we were back to the people we used to be. My injury had brought us back together, and it wasn't until the last session that I realized that none of that was a good thing. My shoulder was feeling better, almost normal, so we decided to stop for an early lunch and celebrate. It seemed innocent, but as soon as we sat down, I realized how dangerous this situation really was.

"To you, Becca, and your full recovery." He lifted his glass and waited for me to do the same in return. I only hesitated a moment before I clinked my water glass to his and took a sip. "So, now that you are free, what are you going to do with all your extra time?"

His question hit a nerve. I was free of therapy, but I was also free of tennis. I hadn't shared with anyone the news that I had received last week. I was still trying to wrap my head around it. My expression must have told him that something was wrong because he reached over the table and grabbed my hand, stroking his thumb over where my ring used to be.

"I can tell that something is going on inside that beautiful brain of yours. Care to share with the rest of the table?"

I tried to pull my hand away put but it was my right hand. He wasn't holding on to me tightly, but he was holding on tight enough that I couldn't muster the strength to break contact. From the look in his eyes, he knew exactly what he was doing.

"I was just thinking that I have a lot to do today at the house and that we should probably eat quickly." The funny thing about lying to someone who knows you as well as Brad knows me is that most of the time it doesn't work. When it does, you can almost see the miracle before you. When he pulled his hand away and waved over the waiter, I think my jaw almost hit the table in disbelief.

On our way to my house after lunch is when things got a little weird. He wasn't talking, the radio was filling the uncomfortable silence for us. Both of his hands were on the steering wheel, and he was gripping it for dear life. Normally, one hand would be on the wheel and the other would be resting on the shifter. He wasn't making eye contact or even glancing in my direction. I'm pretty sure his eyes never left the road in front of him. Not to mention I could feel the tension in the air but I just wasn't sure I wanted to say anything.

About a mile from my house, he pulled the car over and cut the engine. He still hadn't look in my direction and he still wasn't talking, but I could feel the tension mounting, and I knew that things were about to explode. A minute went by with nothing said. Then five. After ten minutes, I was thinking about getting out and walking the rest of the way home. As I was about to pull the handle on the door and let myself out is when he finally spoke.

"When did they tell you?"

I knew what he was eluding to. Playing dumb was the way I decided to go. "Tell me what?"

He did a full body turn in his seat to face me, but didn't say anything for what felt like forever. He knew I was bluffing, and he was done dancing around the subject. He wanted a straight answer from me and was waiting for me to give it to him. *Crap!*

"Last week." It was all I could get out before I broke down and started to cry. I hadn't shed a single tear for myself in over a month, and it felt like the flood gates just opened. Once I started, I wasn't able to stop so we sat there. I'm not sure for how long, but at some point, Brad got out and came around to my side of the car and crawled in the passenger seat with me. He let me cry until I couldn't cry anymore, and then he kissed away my remaining tears on my cheeks, my nose, and then my lips.

Crap!

Chapter Three

My party was a lot of fun. Friends I hadn't seen, people I had been avoiding, and my entire family was there. It was a great day. For a small amount of time, I was able to focus on something other than my shoulder. I was able to laugh freely, engage in meaningless conversations, and just enjoy myself. The only thing that was constantly trying to push its way into my mind were thoughts of Brad. He never showed his face at the party, and I think that he did it purposely.

After cleaning up the next day, Ethan and I went out to dinner to celebrate alone. I wasn't sure what my present was, but I wished he had given it to me last night with all of our friends and family around. It wouldn't have taken any of the surprise away or made it any less special. I would have been able to share my excitement, my joy with everyone else. He doesn't always see things that way so here we are at dinner, the day after my birthday, just so he can give me my present.

The restaurant is filled to capacity as it always is. It's become one of our favorites over the past couple of years, for more reasons than one. First, they take reservations so we never have to wait. Second, their entire dessert menu is chocolate so I never indulge. Don't get me wrong, I love chocolate as much as the next person, but I also know what it does to my figure if I eat it too often. These days, I don't have much to stay in shape for but old habits die hard. Maybe I'll indulge tonight?

Unglued

Finally, everything is tapas. We always order a variety of different things and share. I love tapas restaurants because you are not stuck deciding between entrees. This way I get to have a little Ahi tuna, a little steak, maybe some chicken and the list can go on and on depending on what we order. Plus, with some of the menu being seasonal, they are constantly offering something new almost every time we visit.

Our table is towards the back of the restaurant tonight. It's quiet and cozy, and couldn't be more romantic. It's perfect for my birthday dinner, and reminds me of how much I love Ethan. As much as I hate going out and as much as I hate celebrating these days, he always knows exactly how to lift my mood.

"This is perfect, just like you." I reach across the table and put my hand over his. He intertwines our finger and smiles. His smile reaches his eyes, and even in the dim lighting, I can see his dimple wink at me.

"I'm glad you like it. I called the restaurant last week and had them prepare a few special things for us tonight that I hope you enjoy."

"Really? They can do that?"

"They were able to accommodate me, let's just leave it at that."

"Okay..."

"No questions, lets just enjoy and celebrate you."

Turning twenty-one is a huge milestone for most people. I felt like I turned twenty-one when Ethan did. We no longer had to hunt for people to buy us beer. I no longer felt like I was breaking the law when we had wine with dinner. When Ethan turned twenty-one, it took all the fun out of me turning twenty-one.

Maybe not all the fun. As the waiter approaches our table, I realized that for the first time, I am able to order a drink with my dinner. My face must have lit up because I can see Ethan's dimple winking at me again. I try to hide my smile from the waiter but it didn't work, and when he asks for my ID, I gladly handed over my new license.

"Well, that was different. I forgot that I would be able to have a drink with dinner."

"It's exciting the first time, knowing that your documentation proves that you are legal. Remember how they didn't even card me, and I was practically pushing my license in his hands?"

"Yeah. That was pretty funny." I remember that moment like it happened yesterday, and as I start to laugh, picturing it vividly, the waiter from that night comes to mind. "Oh my god, it's the same waiter, isn't it?"

"Yep. I specifically requested him."

"Why?"

"To teach him a lesson, I guess. I didn't tell his boss that he didn't card me because that could get him in trouble, but I made sure that his boss knew that I wanted him to card you since we were celebrating your twenty-first. I don't think he remembers us."

I could see the waiter trying to make his way back to our table through the crowd. He was holding the tray with our drinks on it above his head, and for a minute I thought that he might spill my wine. I knew that I could order another glass, but this glass was special. He set our drinks down and excused himself. Ethan lifted his glass for a toast and I followed suit. That's when I realized what was going on.

I could barely make it out in the dim lighting but in my heart I knew what was about to happen. The shock on my face registered with Ethan immediately as he dropped to one knee in front of me and grabbed my free hand. I could see in his eyes that he was nervous.

"Yes." I whispered it so softly that I wasn't sure I had even said it. I know that my lips moved and I felt the air that had passed them, but I didn't actually hear myself say anything. Judging by the expression on Ethan's face, he heard me loud and clear.

"You know, I'm supposed to ask you first. You're stealing my thunder here." He's chuckling, but I still can't erase the shock from my face. I want to laugh with him. I want to smile. The only emotion I can feel right now is pure shock.

I forced myself to smile at him, but I still can't muster any words. I am truly speechless. I always thought that someday, we would grow up, get married, settle down, and have a house full of kids (or maybe just two), but I didn't think forever was going to start so soon.

Before I realized what's going on, I can see that he's emptied my wine glass and is pulling the ring from the bottom. He carefully, but quickly, dries it on my napkin and placed it at the tip of my left ring finger. I'm staring at the ring, and he's staring at me.

"Rebecca Blake, will you be my wife?"

"Yes." This time I heard it, and so did he. He slides the ring on my finger just as he kisses me deeply on the lips. I can hear clapping in the background, and even a few whistles. I didn't realize that we had put on a show.

Having dinner after getting engaged is surreal. I remembered ordering a few things and trying them. I remembered toasting to our life ahead. I even remembered asking the couple at the next table to take our picture with my phone. The entire time I felt like I was floating on air. It was as if I was watching the situation from behind a frosted glass window.

When I woke up the next morning, the first thing I did was send my mom a picture of my ring. It was early, about seven, but she called only seconds after I hit send. I'm not sure who was more excited, but I think it may have been her. I could hear my sister yelling at her to be quiet in the background, so I sent the picture to her phone too. I heard her scream when she got the picture, and then she was on the phone instantly.

"Wow! Congratulations, Sis." Amy was practically screaming into the phone. I held it out far enough, away from my ear, that I could still hear her but not go deaf.

"Thanks. I'm pretty excited too."

"Really? You don't sound very excited."

Didn't I? I was excited. I was thrilled. I was surprised. I certainly didn't hesitate when he asked. There wasn't conflicting thoughts going through my head as to what to say. I know I want to spend the rest of my life with him. I am excited.

"I am excited but I think you might be more excited. I've had time to get over the shock and you just found out. Plus, I knew I wanted to marry Ethan. It was just a matter of when, and now I know it will be sooner rather than later."

"Wow! Rationalizing your engagement. You really need to let loose."

"Shut up and let me talk to Mom."

"Fine, but I get to be a bridesmaid."

"Of course. You can stand next to Natalie. Now can I please talk to Mom?"

"Sure. Love you."

"You too." As I waited for my mom to jump back on the line, I started to picture my wedding. Who was going to be in it? Who was my maid of honor? Where would we get married? What would I wear? What part would Brad play in all of it?

"*Hello!*"

"Sorry, Mom, lost in thought. So, are you okay with this? I don't think he asked you or Dad, and I know that's old-fashioned, but it still matters that we have your blessing."

"He asked both of us a while ago, so yes, you have our blessing."

"What? When?"

"Well, I'll let you ask him that."

"Fine. I have to study for an exam. Are you still coming over on Saturday night for Brad's party?"

"We will be there. Have you told him yet?"

"No, but I will see him between classes tomorrow so I can tell him then."

"Okay, sweetie, good luck."

"Everything will be fine. He should have seen this coming, and I know he'll be okay with it. Right?"

"I don't know that he'll be okay with it, but he will find a way to accept it in time. That boy loves you almost as much as Ethan, maybe more."

"It's a different kind of love, Mom."

"You're right, it is different. It's also deeper than any love I've ever seen. Don't get me wrong, I know that Ethan loves you and that you love him, but Brad's love is different, and as much as I want the two of you to stay friends forever, this might be the straw that breaks the camel's back."

She was right. He was gonna flip out on me. I have to tell him, it's not an option, but I don't know how. This could be the end of our friendship. I have finally chosen Ethan over Brad, for good. There was no chance for me to change my mind once we were married.

"Thanks, Mom. I gotta go."

"Okay. Call me later if you want. Love you."

"Love you too."

I immediately dial Natalie's number, hoping to catch her before she heads to work. I know that I need someone to talk to. I need someone to rationalize the situation with me. I need someone to tell me that Brad will take the news just fine. Natalie will be that person. She's always that person. She's the one that keeps us all moving forward. She's the glue that keeps us all from falling apart.

Voicemail. *Crap!*

I didn't leave a message. I stared at my phone, wondering who I can call now. I could just call Brad and break the news to him tonight. I contemplated that idea for less than a second when my phone rings, and Ella's smiling face is staring at me. Perfect!

"Hello."

"Becca! How are you?"

"Good. Great actually. I was just about to call you. How are you?"

"I'm doing great. I'm actually calling because I have some news."

"Really? I have some news too. You go first."

"Okay. Well, I'm engaged!"

"Congrats! Me too!"

"Seriously? Congrats!"

Amazing. Ella had a hard time getting over Brad, but it never affected our relationship. I stayed out of it. When she moved back home to Michigan, it was almost like we became closer. She never told me what happened between them and I never asked. After a few months, she met a guy named Luke, and started dating him. Brad was long forgotten at that point.

"I'm so happy for you, Ella. Luke is a good guy, and a very lucky one if you ask me."

"Yeah. So, Ethan finally asked you, huh? It took him long enough."

"Um, it's been less than five years, which was the original plan in my mind."

"Yeah, but he bought that ring almost a year ago. I was beginning to wonder if something was going on that you weren't telling me about."

What? Ethan bought my ring that long ago? I was confused.

"Nope. Things are great." At least they were until five seconds ago.

"So, is that why you were calling?"

"Yes and no." Okay, just ask her what she thinks. She knows Brad as well as I do, maybe better since she dated him.

"So, what's up then? I can hear it in your voice. You're not second guessing your decision are you?"

"No! I love Ethan. I want to marry him." I was talking louder than I wanted to. Ethan was in the house somewhere. He was possibly closer than I knew. I needed to keep that in mind.

"Then what's up with the uncertainty in your voice?"

"Well, I was hoping you might help me out with something?"

"Okay?"

"Well, I haven't told Brad yet and—"

"*No!* I will not tell him for you."

"Not exactly what I was going to say. I would never ask you to do that for me. I was just wondering if I could ask you a question about him, but we never talk about him so I wasn't sure if you would be okay with it."

I was rambling. I knew I was but I couldn't help it. I was nervous. What if she didn't want to talk about him?

"Oh. That's fine. What's up?"

"Well, my mom seems to think that my engagement will cause some tension in our relationship. I know that Brad and I have a very different relationship, but I think he will be fine once he gets use to the idea. What do you think?"

I can hear her breathing. She's quiet for a while and just as I'm about to say something, wondering if maybe she hung up at some point, she finally answers me.

"I think that it's time to tell you why Brad and I broke up."

Oh Crap!

This cannot be good. I don't know if I want to hear this. I don't know if I can handle this. Like he knew I needed someone to rescue me, Ethan walks into the room and tells me that breakfast is ready.

I quickly got off the phone with Ella, promising to call her as soon as I tell Brad.

Chapter four

Studying was the last thing I was able to do last night. The only thing I could think about was how to "break the news" to Brad that Ethan and I were engaged. After overanalyzing the situation over and over again, I came to the conclusion that he was gonna freak out.

I was well aware of the fact that our relationship was "unconventional" at best. I was aware that he probably still held feelings for me, and that those feelings were going to be crushed once he found out that I was marrying Ethan. I was also aware that deep down, I was still holding onto feelings for him.

That was the part that scared me the most. I knew that those feelings were there. I knew because I was still constantly reminding myself to repress them. Every time they try to surface, I spend the day reminding myself of all the reasons that I love Ethan, all the reasons that my friendship with Brad is better than any relationship we could ever have, and all the reasons that I don't want either of those things to change.

I love him deeply. I don't know any other way to love him. I don't want to love him any other way. I want my love for him to be a part of me, always. I just don't want my love for him to define who I am and the decisions that I make. That's part of why I chose Ethan back in high school. I felt free when I was with him. Free to love unconditionally.

My love for Ethan never tried to define who I was or who I should have been. I was just me. The love that I had for him back then, that I tried to show him in every way possible, was cherished. He knew that I expected nothing in return, but yet he gave more than I ever expected. He loved me back.

I know that marrying Ethan is the right decision. I know that I will be happy with him, for the rest of my life. I also know that Brad will never see it that way. No matter how many times over the years I have tried to tell him, tried to show him, that my love for him is different than my love for Ethan, he never once seemed to grasp it. Maybe he just didn't want to. I have a weakness when it comes to him. My heart weakens around him and he knows it.

My first class of the day went by much faster than I wanted it to. It's amazing how when you want time to slow down, it does the opposite. All I wanted today was for time to slow down, just a little. I needed time to formulate a plan, to figure out what to say, how to say it. All I could think about was how he was going to react.

It's not like time was going to change things. No matter when I told him or how I told him, his reaction was going to be the same. He was going to be disappointed. I know that as a friend, he should be elated for me. Maybe elated was a stretch. I would settle for happy. I would settle for a meaningless congratulations at this point.

Leaving my class, all I could feel was an overwhelming sense of dread. I had so much going on this month that adding this into the mix was starting to complicate things. Brad's birthday was Thursday and we were supposed to be celebrating at our house on Saturday night. If he wasn't able to accept our engagement… well, I just don't know what's going to happen. Would he cancel his party? Would we still have it as planned?

Rounding the building, I catch sight of him waiting for me on the bench outside the cafeteria. I stop dead in my tracks and just stare. My body is trembling in fear. The anticipation is overwhelming, and I'm not sure if I can bring myself to tell him. It all seemed feasible when he wasn't standing in front of me, but now I'm not sure what to do, what to say, or how to say it. I've never been afraid to tell him anything, until now.

Just the thought of losing him scares me to death. He's been a part of my life for so long that I can't imagine him not being in it. I've let my guard down around him, more than I should, and allowed him in. It's not the same as what I have with Ethan. Ethan has always been important to me. We fought the odds to be together, but it feels like I've been fighting an internal battle ever since. I was only weak once, but it happened, and it changed things.

I broke the kiss and pulled back. I had stopped crying a while ago and let Brad take over. Kissing him made me forget all the bad crap that was going on around me. Kissing him was also wrong. I knew that when I kissed him back, but for some reason, those thoughts didn't stop it from happening.

His eyes are as dark as I've ever seen them. The specks of gold around his irises are barely visible, and he's breathing so deeply that I can feel his chest against mine every time he inhales. I know that look. I've seen it a few times, but not recently. I've been avoiding it for the past few years, and I should have been trying to avoid it right now.

"We shouldn't be doing this. It's wrong. We both know that."

I knew that I sounded unsure. Maybe I am a little. I needed to catch my breath, and I needed to do that with more space between us. His body is blocking me from the door, so I slid across the center console and into the driver's seat.

He rests his cheek on the back of the seat and just stares at me. His breathing is slowly returning to normal, but the look in his eye is not changing. The space I've created between us is not enough. I needed to get out of the car. I needed to get some distance between us before my body starts to tell my brain what to do again.

As I crawled out of the driver's seat, I knew that Brad would do the same. When I reached the front of the car, he's already there waiting for me. He pulls me into a tight embrace and kisses me on the forehead. It's his way of saying he's sorry, but I know that he's probably not as sorry as he should be. It's not like this happens every day. It hasn't happened since we were in high school, but I know that if I allowed it to happen more often, then it would.

"Let's get you home. We can talk there."

He's not going to let this go. I don't really want to talk about tennis. I don't really want to talk about therapy. I *don't* want to talk about what just happened. What's left to talk about? Do I have a choice in the matter? Maybe he will just drop me off.

As soon as we pulled in my driveway, I realized that Ethan is not home from class yet. Without asking, Brad shuts off the car and follows me to the front door. I dropped my purse on the table and went into the kitchen to get a drink. I pulled two bottles of water from the fridge and find Brad standing outside on the patio, staring at the mountains.

I handed him a water and plopped down on the lounge chair. After a few minutes, I realized that Brad's still staring at the mountains, and I'm beginning to wonder if he's ever going to say anything. Not that I really want to talk about anything, but if he's going to make me talk, let's get it over with.

"So, what exactly do you think we need to talk about?"

"Well, there are a number of things, but let's start with what your therapist told you."

Great. Maybe I should have just let him stare off a little longer and kept quiet.

"Okay. He said that my chances of playing tennis again were about one in a million. My range of motion in my shoulder is not getting better, and with the way the bones healed, it's unlikely that it will ever get better. I can continue to go to therapy once a week and hope for the best, or I can give up tennis and try to live a normal life."

"Can you do that? Live a normal life without being able to play tennis?"

That was the real question that I didn't want to answer. Can I become a normal person without tennis? It's always been a part of who I am. It's never defined me as a person, but I've also never been without it. I've never been told that it's not an option. After my first injury, they told me that I would have to work hard to be able to play as well as I had before my injury. I worked so hard that I think I may have gotten better. I used that to motivate me.

Now what?

"I can try, I guess."

"What about your scholarship?"

"I have to have a release form to be able to play and I won't get one, so I will lose my scholarship. I have to talk to my mom to see if she can help pay for tuition, and I'm probably going to have to get a part-time job."

So that was that. I was done with tennis, at least on a competitive level. Maybe someday, I would be able to play for fun again, but with the way my shoulder feels on most days, it was unlikely. Silence from Brad meant that he understood completely. It's not like I was dying, but a part of me was—a big part.

"So, can I ask you something?"

"Of course."

I was tentative with my answer. I knew that I wasn't going to like the question, but I knew that I would have to answer it eventually. It was inevitable, and since Ethan wasn't home, now was probably the best time.

"What happened between us?"

Not what I was expecting.

"Um, I'm not sure what you're asking. Do you mean a few minutes ago?"

"No. I mean a few years ago."

"I'm not sure. I didn't realize that something happened."

"Things changed. After you came here, it was like you became a different person."

"Good or bad different? I didn't realize that I had changed that much."

"Good and bad. My best friend was always someone who was there for me, and you were, most of the time. Then you started to date Ethan and things changed."

"Nothing changed. I started dating and you didn't want me to at first. In fact, I specifically remember you trying to date me to keep me from dating him. Then, you gave him your blessing, and the rest seems like history, right?"

"I gave him my blessing to take care of you, to watch over you. I didn't give him permission to fall in love with you, or for you to fall in love with him."

"*Excuse me*! I'm pretty sure that I don't need permission to fall in love, and that when I fell in love with Ethan, was before you gave him 'permission' to take care of me."

"That's not what I meant and you know it. I'm not trying to run your life; I just want to be a part of it, and it feels like you've shut me out of parts of your life. Don't you see that?"

"No, I don't. What I see is you trying to get in between my

relationship with Ethan by kissing me and confusing me."

As soon as his head whipped towards me, I knew that I shouldn't have said that. Admitting to myself that kissing Brad confused me is one thing, but admitting it to Brad was another and was a mistake. He was never supposed to know.

"One more question and then I have to go."

He's moving towards me and I'm paralyzed by the look in his eyes. My body feels heavy, and as much as I want to sit up and move away, I can't. My body won't cooperate. It's like his stare has put me in a trance, and not in the good kind of way. The only thing I can do is nod, so I do, giving him permission to continue.

"Do you know how much I love you?"

Do I know how much he loves me? Of course I do. Do I want to admit to myself how much he loves me? *Absolutely not!* Do I want to admit to myself how much I love him? I never have, out loud at least, and I never will. It's a part of me that will die with me at this point.

I've been standing in this spot for almost ten minutes, and I still don't have the courage to go over and tell him. Maybe I should just avoid it altogether. I can send him a text and tell him that I can't meet him for coffee today. He would understand, right?

As I pulled out my phone to chicken out, I realized that he had already sent me a text. Here's my chance. I can just tell him that I forgot that we were meeting and his text reminded me. Perfect! I was getting out of this with an even better lie.

Brad: R U going to stand there all day or are we getting coffee?

Crap!

He saw me standing here, and instead of walking over, he let me stand here looking like an idiot. When did he send this? Five minutes ago. Great! Now I really look like an idiot. He's going to know that something is up. He's gonna ask questions, and I'm not going to be able to avoid answering them. I cannot lie to him. I can, just not very well and he knows it every time.

As gracefully as possible, I put my phone back in my purse and walked over to where he's waiting. I try to act like nothing is wrong but as I approached him, I realized that I was twisting my ring. He's bound to notice, and before he does, I slipped it off my finger and into my pocket.

What? Why did I just do that?

I'm not going to be able to avoid this conversation forever. It's best to get it out of the way now. I want to be the one to tell him. I don't want him to hear it from one of our friends. I don't want him to find out at his party. I especially don't want Ethan to be the one to tell him. If Ethan tells him, then Ethan will know that I didn't tell him and will wonder why. I don't need Ethan wondering why I didn't tell him. I don't need him questioning whether or not I really want to marry him.

"Hey. For a minute there I thought you were never going to join me."

I give him a quick hug and apologize for being late. He guides me through the open doors and into the cafeteria. I can feel his hand on the small of my back through my sweatshirt, and my body betrays me by reacting with a shiver. I know he noticed and is probably smiling at the way he can always get to me, whether I like it or not.

I find us a table while he grabs our coffee. The place is pretty empty for being a week before finals. Next week, it will be packed with students trying to get a pick-me-up from caffeine in between studying and taking exams. There won't be an available table, and we will probably have to grab our coffee and sit outside. I'll have to remember to bring a coat next week.

"So," he says as he places my coffee in front of me, "what was that all about? You looked like you were somewhere deep inside your head while you were staring at me."

I was staring? *Crap!*

"Nothing. Just going through my to-do list. I didn't see you at first, so I was just waiting." Two lies. Will he believe me?

"Sure you were." Nope. Not gonna buy it. "What is really on your mind?"

"Nothing. Why?"

"Well, I just happen to run into Ethan this morning and he asked if I had talked to you lately. I told him we were having coffee today and that I would see you then. He seemed surprised that I hadn't talked to you. Is there something you're not telling me?"

"No, of course not." Unless you count the fact that I got engaged over the weekend. "He was probably wondering if I had yelled at you for not coming to my party on Friday."

"I did come, though. I take it you didn't tell him I was there?"

"No, and thank you for the present. It's beautiful."

"Just like you." I know that I was starting to blush so I looked away and tried to focus on what was going on outside. I could see a couple making out under a tree but it felt wrong to stare. "So, why are you not wearing it? It's going to look beautiful on your wrist."

"It will."

"What's wrong, Becca? I can tell that there's something that you're not telling me so out with it. You should know better than to try to keep things from me after all this time." He's smiling as he says it, but only because he knows it's true. I can't keep anything from him, as much as I would like to sometimes.

"I just…well…I don't really know how to tell you this."

"Just say it. It can't be that bad, can it?"

"Well, Ethan and I…we…well, we sort of…"

"Sort of what, Becca? Are you pregnant?"

Okay, that was said much louder than it needed to be. I don't know everyone on campus but I know a lot of people, and that is the last thing I need people spreading around.

"No! I'm not pregnant. Thanks for whispering that by the way."

"Then what?"

"Well, Ethan asked me to marry him."

From the silence that followed, I knew that he was in shock. His face was void of all emotion, but his body was telling a different story. I could see it start to tense up, and I knew that he wanted to explode. I'm not sure why he was angry, but I knew that was what his reaction was at that moment. As the seconds ticked by and I waited for him to say something, I could see that he was trying to calm himself down. After a few minutes, the tension was gone, and he looked like he had before I broke the news to him.

"Well, what did you say?" His eyes finally left mine and flew to my hands that were wrapped around my coffee cup. I knew they were missing a key piece of jewelry, but he didn't. He really didn't know yet. I had to tell him.

Moment of truth. "Yes. I said yes."

He was gone before I could say anything else. The loss I felt when the therapist told me that I would never play tennis again was nothing compared to the overwhelming pain in my chest right now. It felt like someone had tried to rip out my heart. It was at that moment that I knew I had lost his friendship forever. Everything was going to change.

Crap!

Chapter five

I gave Brad Tuesday to cool off. I needed to sort out the details of his party, if there was going to be one now. We had already sent out e-vites to all of our friends, but I knew that there were a few people that still needed to be informed. I didn't want to wait until the last minute. I was going shopping for food and alcohol on Thursday, so I knew that I needed to talk to him soon, but he needed a day.

I wasn't expecting him to show up for coffee on Wednesday. He was waiting for me as usual and I was caught off guard. Was he still upset? I knew that the engagement was a shock to him but it really shouldn't have been. With Ethan a week away from graduation, he should have suspected that he would want to start the next phase of his life. If I had been paying attention, I would have thought about it. Maybe I would have been more prepared and seen it coming.

I tentatively approached him. His back was to me, but I knew that he was aware I was there. No matter how distant we have been lately, he would always know when I walked in to a room, and vice versa. It's like we are one person sometimes.

Without turning around, he started to speak. I wasn't sure if he was avoiding eye contact or if he was ashamed, but when I went to stand in front of him, he turned the other direction. His voice was no louder than a whisper and I was having hard time hearing him, so I sat down next to him and took his hand in mine. This caught his attention and his eyes immediately met mine.

"I'm so sorry."

"I know you are and I'm not mad at you."

"You should be." He broke eye contact again and it was as if he was still in pain. I could tell that something was troubling him, and I was pretty sure that I knew what it was.

"Look. We need to lay everything out on the table and get past this. We have your birthday this week, and I want to make sure your party is the best one yet. We still have a lot to talk about so let's get our coffee and talk. Okay?"

"Becca." He was whispering again. The pain in his voice was overwhelming, and when I felt him touch my cheek, I turned toward his hand and closed my eyes instead of moving away. That was my first mistake. My second was not stopping him from kissing me. The third, the one I'll never understand, is not stopping myself from kissing him back.

When my brain finally started working again, I pulled away. He had tears in his eyes, and I'm pretty sure that I had them in mine. I felt everything he was trying to say to me. I knew— without him having to say a word—that he was going to fight to have me as his own. I felt the love in that one kiss and it scared the hell out of me.

Instead of talking about it, I stood up and walked into the cafeteria. Once I had our coffees, I made my way back out to where Brad was still sitting. He took the coffee from me but didn't say a word. That's how we spent the next half hour. Sitting in comfortable silence. There were no words that would help us figure out our situation. There was nothing that could be said that would solve any of the turmoil that I was about to put myself through.

When I got home that afternoon, I knew that I needed to talk to Ethan. I was sure that I wanted to marry him, but I wasn't sure that I wanted to marry him right now. I still wanted to finish college. I still wanted to travel before starting a career. I wanted to explore and have fun and then get married, start a career, and eventually, start a family.

He was waiting for me in the living room. I could feel the negative energy when I crossed the threshold. Something was wrong with him, and I wasn't quite sure what it was. I was scared to test the waters with what I had to say. I knew that whatever was going on with him today, that I would make things worse if I were to bring up any of my concerns or insecurities about us.

"Hey," I said to him as I slowly approached where he was sitting.

"Hey." It came out in a huff, and that's when I knew something was seriously wrong.

"Bad day?"

"You could say that. It's not every day you get fired."

"What? The evil bitch fired you? Why?"

"She said that I was no longer needed, and that they were going to be eliminating my position. It's a load of bull and I know it. She's been trying to get rid of me for a while now."

"Well, that's her loss. If she can't appreciate your hard work and talent then someone else will." For this I was granted a smile. Not a big one, his dimple was still in hiding, but it was a start.

"How was your day?"

"It was fine." Crap! I shouldn't have said fine. I should have said good. Fine is like a conversation starter for all details of one's day. I don't want to rehash my weird morning.

"Just fine, huh? Did you have coffee with Brad?"

"Yeah. He was in a mood, so we didn't get to work out all the details for his party, so I guess I am just going to have to figure it out on my own. Do you want to go shopping with me tomorrow when I get home?" I knew he would be free since he wasn't going to have to go to work now. This would give me an opportunity to gauge when he expects us to tie the knot.

"Sure."

Just as we were settling in for the night, I heard my phone ting with a text message. I went to grab it, but there was nothing there. I heard another ting and realized that it was Ethan's phone and not mine. Who would be texting him so late? I picked it up to take it to him, and the screen turned on showing that his incoming text was from his former boss. Huh?

I know that I shouldn't invade his privacy, but there was no way I was going to pass up the opportunity to tell this woman to stick it. I slid the unlock key and found that he had six new texts and they were all from her. The first was from this afternoon, right before he told me that he got fired. Let's see what she had to say.

Unglued

Can u please come over so I can explain?

Explain? What is she talking about? If you fire someone, that pretty much sums up everything that you need to talk about.

Ethan, please call me.

Why won't you just call me? I can explain everything.

Ethan, it's a great opportunity, you should take it.

What opportunity? It doesn't sound like he's been fired. What the hell is going on?

Ethan, they need an answer by tomorrow lunch. You need to call me.

If this is about your gf then you need to get over it. She will understand if she really loves you.

If what is about me? I'm his fiancée, not his girlfriend. Why doesn't she know this? What opportunity is she talking about? I cannot believe that she's sent him six texts today, and he hasn't mentioned to me anything about this.

My body starts to tingle, and I immediately know that I have been busted. He can't be more than four feet behind me, and there is no way that I will be able to put his phone back without him noticing. Can I put it in the front of my pants and return it later? That's what I'll do. I'll stick it in the elastic band on my shorts and hope that he doesn't notice or catch me.

Ting

Crap!

"Becca, do you have my phone?"

"Yeah. I was bringing it to you when the screen lit up. It was your boss so I was going to text her something mean, but instead I read the text she sent you." I don't want to turn around and face the wrath of what might happen. I know that he would never hit me, but I also know that this is going to make him angrier than I have ever seen him. I invaded his privacy. I would be upset if he did it to me yet I did it anyway.

"So, can I have my phone then?" There's a hint of anger in his voice, but not as much as I expected.

I turned around slowly and handed him his phone. He scrolls through his text messages and reads each one. You can see that they bothered him. You can see that he's angry, but I'm pretty sure it's with his boss and not with me.

"So, I guess you're wondering what she wants."

"Yeah. I thought you were fired."

"I was. They offered me another position but I turned it down. When my boss heard, she fired me, so that I would take the other job. She thought that she was going to force me into taking it."

"What? They offered you a different position? Why didn't you take it?"

"There are a bunch of reasons."

"Is it because of me? She made it sound like it was because of me, and I don't want you to hold yourself back because of me. Whatever it is, we will find a way to deal with it."

"It's not because of you, Becca. It's for you. It's for us. Our life. If I take that job, then things will change, and I can't do it without you." There is a hint of uncertainty in his voice. For a moment I think that maybe, just maybe, he thinks I will leave him.

"Then we'll do it together. Do I even get a vote?"

"If you really want one, then you do."

"I agreed to marry you because I want to spend the rest of my life with you. That life starts now. Every decision that needs to be made, we can make together. Deal?"

Crap! What about waiting to get married? Wasn't I just having a conversation with myself about wanting to do all these other things before jumping into marriage?

"Deal. So, how do you feel about England?"

"Um, I don't know. What does England have to do with work?"

England? What? Where is he going with this? I've never been to England, not by choice. I would love to visit and see the sights. Is that what this is about? Did they offer him an opportunity to work in England? For how long?

"Well, they are opening a gallery in England, and they want me to run it."

"Wow! That's a big promotion. Would you still be able to shoot pictures for the company, or would this be it for you? Would you be choosing the art instead of producing it?" I tried to contain my excitement for him but it was overwhelming. This is such a great opportunity for him. Why does he not sound more excited?

"I would be doing both. They want to give me all the creative decision-making power over there. I would be able to discover new artists, and showcase their work. I would also be able to showcase some of my own work."

"Why you?"

"Well, they think I can do it. They know that I'm graduating next week, and with a degree in photo journalism and a minor in business, they think that I can handle it. Of course, I would hire people to do some of the business stuff but, the artistic aspect of it is all me."

I can hear the excitement in his voice now. I know he wants to do this. I know he wants to take this job. He should take this job. What about us? What will I do while he's over in England running his gallery? I still have three semesters of school to finish. I can't just up and leave.

"Becca. Where did you go? You zoned out on me for a minute."

"I was just thinking about what a great opportunity it is for you."

"For us. I won't go unless you agree to go with me. I can't imagine doing this without you."

"I can't go, Ethan. I still have to finish school."

"What if you deferred a semester and come back this summer. Just give it one semester over there, and you can decide if you want to stay, or come back and finish school. School's always going to be here, Becca." I can see that he doesn't want to try and push me into this but that he wants me to make my own decision. "What do you think?"

Ting

His damn phone needs to be turned off right now. If his boss would give us time to sort through all of this, then maybe she would get her answer tomorrow. I need to sleep on it. I need to weigh all my options. Could I do a study abroad?

Ting

"Just tell her that you will have an answer for her tomorrow so she stops texting you." I'm irritated by her right now and a little overwhelmed. I didn't mean to snap at him.

"That was your phone."

I reached around him and grabbed my phone off of the bed. I had two new texts. As I opened them up, I felt faint. I knew that this moment was coming, but I didn't think it would be right now. I don't know how much more life-altering news I can take right now.

Brad: I love you Becca but since you are engaged, I think it would be best if I distance myself.

Brad: Cancel the party.

Crap! This cannot be happening. I went to toss my phone on the bed but Ethan grabs it out of my hand. Before I can stop him, he's reading the words on the screen. I can see the anger in his eyes. I can feel the tension in the room. My breathing has become erratic and I feel faint. Then that's what I do. I faint.

Chapter Six

We never talked about the text from Brad. In fact, I think fainting took his mind off of everything. When I finally came around, he was holding a cool washcloth to my forehead, and my body was curled in his lap. I don't think he knew I was awake because he was still talking to himself. I couldn't make out what he was saying but I knew that it didn't matter. No matter what words were coming out, the only thing that mattered was the fact that he was here.

I shifted my weight and he removed the washcloth. I could see the panic in his eyes. I could feel the tension in his body as I pushed off of him and got to my feet. He followed my lead and stood as well. Walking over to the dresser, I picked up my phone and opened a new text. I typed quickly and hit Send before he could reach me. The moment his phone went off, he looked at me, confusion now shining brightly from his eyes.

Me: I would love to move to England with you.

The next thing I knew, I was being pulled into his arms, my feet were in the air, and we were spinning in circles. I could feel the bile rising in my throat. I pushed away from Ethan, and stumbled towards our bathroom, opening the lid to the toilet just as I expelled my dinner. I heaved up the rest of the contents of my stomach, and when I felt like

Unglued

I wasn't nauseated anymore, I stood up. I quickly brushed my teeth, rinsed with mouthwash, and headed back into our room.

I knew he was going to want to talk about the job. I knew he was going to want to talk about me leaving school. I was the one who normally overanalyzed everything. This time, I knew it would be him. This was a big step. Not just for our relationship, but for our future. Without tennis, there really wasn't anything stopping me from leaving. That's when thoughts of Brad started to creep back into my mind.

He had moved across the country to be closer to me. He had uprooted his whole life to be closer to me. He never gave up on our friendship. He never gave up on me. He wanted to be with me, and this was going to be the distance that our relationship needed. He was the reason that I wanted to leave. He was also the reason that I wanted to stay. I didn't want to leave him, again.

"So, I guess we're moving to England?" It was a question. I know that he was excited and was trying to hide it, but he was doing a poor job. His dimple was winking at me, and the smile on his face was anything but tentative while he awaited my answer.

"Yes. We're moving to England. Now, will you please text your boss so that we can be left alone for the night." There went his smile. Crap! I shouldn't have brought up the texts. I could see the change in his demeanor. His body went rigid, and his eyes glossed over. He tossed me a small smile, trying to reassure me I guess, before he grabbed his phone and walked out of the room. I took the opportunity to text Brad as quickly as I could.

Me: We need to talk. Meet me 2moro for coffee at noon.

It didn't take long for my phone to ting. Crap! I turned the volume off on my phone before reading his message. I didn't want Ethan to know that while he was accepting a job, I was in here talking to Brad. It just didn't feel right. We needed time to discuss everything.

Brad: Cant busy

Me: Bull important pls be there

Brad: No

Me: Don't make this harder than it has to be

A few minutes went by and nothing came back from him. I was baiting him and he wasn't taking the bait. I could hear that Ethan was now on the phone talking to someone. I slipped into the bathroom and waited. When he still hadn't gotten back to me after almost five minutes, I gave up completely. I was going to have to stalk him tomorrow to get him to talk to me, if he would talk to me. Or at least that was my plan until my phone vibrated in my hand.

Brad: It's already hard. Go to England and be happy

What? How the hell did he know that? Did Ethan tell him? Did Ethan texted him? Was that who he was talking to? I needed to know what was going on, and just as I was about to open the door, it opened for me. With his phone still in his hand, he gave me a slight smile. I could see the victory in his eyes. He knew he had won, but I wasn't a prize.

"What did you do?"

"I called him and told him that we were moving to England. Now, he doesn't have to create space between you guys. Half of the country and the entire Atlantic will be separating you from him, and that will give him plenty of time and space to get over whatever he needs to get over."

"Seriously. How can you be so crude? He's my best friend. Don't you think that I wanted to be the one to tell him that we were moving?"

"He can't be your best friend right now. He's in love with you. He's blinded by that love. I think he's more upset that you're leaving than he is about us getting engaged."

"Probably because he came here to be closer to me."

Crap!

That's when it hit me. There was nothing holding Brad here but me. There was no reason for him to stay here except for me. The only reason he was here was because of me. He's tried to tell me, tried to show me. He wants to be here because he wants to be with me. He made the "ultimate sacrifice" a long time ago, and has been patiently waiting for me to realize.

Unglued

It's like Ethan knew that I needed time to let this all sink in. He excused himself and went to take a shower. I heard the water turn on, and I heard him close the curtain. I was still holding my cell phone in my hand, and it was blinking, alerting me to a waiting text. I knew it was going to be from Brad, but I wasn't sure if I wanted to know what he had to say. Against my better judgment, I opened it and my mouth hit the floor.

Brad: I love you. I have always loved you and I will always love you and if you go to England with Ethan then I will never be able to show you how much I love you. If you marry him then I will never be able to show you how much I love you. look in your heart Becca and tell me that you don't love me and I will walk away but I need for you to say the words cuz I know that deep down you love me as much as I love you

Crap! Crap! Crap!
I immediately deleted our entire conversation. I don't want Ethan to see that text. I don't want to re-read that text. I don't want to think about that text. The last time he told me he loved me, I knew that he was speaking from the heart. I knew that he wasn't talking about a crush like he had in high school. I knew that it was more than a simple physical attraction. It was the kind of love that scared the crap out of me. I avoided him for almost a week afterwards because I was afraid of what else he might confess to. I was afraid that he would lay all his cards out on the table like he just did in that text.

The text may have been deleted, but it was still fresh in my mind as I drifted off to sleep. Ethan had his arms wrapped protectively around me, but that didn't stop me from dreaming of Brad.

"Of course I know how much you love me." I do know but I try to ignore it most of the time. His love is powerful and all-consuming and scares the crap out of me. "You're my best friend, Brad. I love you too."

He quickly looked away, and I knew that I had just shut him down in the best way I possibly could. Every time he has tried to "profess his undying love for me," I have shut him down by throwing our friendship in his face. If I let him say what he felt, if I let him continue telling me all the things that he wants to tell me, I would be in a bunch of trouble, because as much as I would like to think that I would be able to resist his advances, the incident in the car is proof that I wouldn't be able to.

He's staring at me again, or maybe just towards me. He's got a blank look in his eye, and I can't really tell what he's thinking. I know that he wants to say something, but I'm just not sure what it's going to be. Whatever it is, he better make it quick. I can hear Ethan shutting his car door, and that means that he's about to lose his chance in the next sixty seconds.

"Just say it, whatever it is."

"Do you really want to hear it? Can you handle the complete, uncensored truth?"

"Probably not, but you need to say it. You've been holding back for a while now, and I know that it's getting in the way of our friendship. Just say it, Brad."

"Fine. I love you, Becca. Not like the kind of love that comes and goes, but the forever kind of love. The 'I want to marry you and grow old with you' kind of love. The kind of love that hasn't faded over the last five years but grown stronger. It makes me want to fight for you, for us. I can't do that, though. I can't fight for something that is completely one-sided. Problem is, I think you feel the same way, and I won't do anything about it until you tell me you do."

I'm pretty sure that my jaw hit the ground. He was right in so many ways and wrong in so many others. I love him, deeply. I also love Ethan, deeply. My heart is not conflicted by any means. I am with Ethan because I am in love with Ethan. I am with Ethan because I can see myself with him in ten years, twenty years. Can I see myself with Brad twenty years from now?

Crap!

I can feel Ethan's presence before he even steps out onto the patio. I'm still in a bit of shock, but I quickly shake it off and throw him a big smile. He bends down and gives me a quick peck on the lips and then turns his attention to Brad.

"How is our patient today? Giving you any problems?"

"Nope. It was the last session, so I will let her tell you all about it.

I'm gonna get going."

He gave me a small, forced smile, and then he was gone. I was still sitting in shock, trying my best to hide it from Ethan, unsure if I was able to speak or not. When Ethan came and sat down on the lounger with me, I knew that he was going to start asking questions. Questions about tennis and therapy. Not questions about Brad.

"So, what did your therapist have to say? I can tell by the look on your face that it's not the best news."

"Nope. I probably won't be able to play again, at least not professionally. He won't release me to play, so I will have to forfeit my scholarship." I think I may have still be in shock because the words came out without any emotion behind them, and I was surprised that I didn't start to cry.

Stunned silence. He didn't have the words to make me feel better and he knew it. There was nothing that anyone could say or do to change the fact that I was done with tennis. A part of my life was over. A part of who I was, who I've always been, the part of me that has always been a constant in my life. That's when I started to cry. Relief washed over Ethan's face as he moved me into his lap and held me.

We didn't talk about tennis after that day. The racquets, mine and his, went into the closet in the spare bedroom, locked away until I could face what was really happening. I knew it would be a while before I would be able to look at my racquet and not cry. It would be a while before I could watch my favorite player on television and not want to throw something. My anger was strong, but my resolve to get past it was stronger. At least I hoped it was.

After a few months, I realized that my shoulder was still nowhere near normal, and some of my everyday tasks were complicated by my lack of range of motion. We decided against me getting a part-time job, and instead, Ethan found a new job that paid better. He must have been lucky the day he went out job hunting. He was hired on the spot by a company that wasn't even hiring. Apparently, his portfolio spoke for itself, and they created a position for him in their photography department.

The company was still rather new to Tucson, but was known worldwide for discovering new talent. They had only opened an office and gallery about a year earlier, and relied heavily on the local artists to bring in pieces for their gallery shows. Ethan's job was primarily to shoot photographs for their mailers, magazine, and any advertisement materials.

It was a great job, in the beginning. The first month or so, before he started his last semester of school, he was working forty hours a week and loving his job. Once classes began, he was less than enthusiastic about his job, his boss, and the work that they were asking him to do.

Every day he came home in a bad mood. At first I felt like it was my fault. On more than one occasion, I offered to find a job so that he didn't have to work as much. He always told me that he was fine working and going to class, but I knew different. It put a huge strain on our relationship and as much as we both tried to ignore it, a huge strain on our friendship.

About a month into the semester, he decided to have a talk with his boss. She listened and took to heart everything he said. His workload was lightened and his hours were cut back. Her attitude however, did not change. She was negative at every turn and was never supportive. She made Ethan's job a living hell to go to every day and most days he wanted to quit.

Chapter Seven

I awoke with a start the next morning. Five more minutes and my alarm would have gone off, but it was my phone vibrating that brought me out of my dream. It was a good dream, I think. I know that I woke up smiling but I wasn't sure why.

Another vibration and I am completely awake. I reach for my phone to see that I have a missed call and a new text. The text came first, around one in the morning, from Brad. I can only imagine what he wanted. Against my better judgment—I had yet to have any coffee—I opened the text and read the babble that I could barely make out.

Brad: I lv you we nede to talk plsea call me

I can only imagine he was drunk when he sent it. It doesn't matter. I was planning on finding him on campus today, and we were going to talk. There was a lot said last night that needed to be cleared up sooner rather than later. I didn't want to lose him. I didn't want to lose our friendship. I did love him.

After throwing on my robe, I turned off my alarm before it hit seven thirty and slipped out of the bedroom. Ethan is still fast asleep, snoring lightly. I know that he's a heavy sleeper, but I walked on my tiptoes even after I left the room just in case he's on the verge of waking up. I need coffee before my day gets any more complicated.

I set the machine to brew and grab my phone off the counter. I dial in to my voicemail and wait. I can hear an operator on the other end of the line talking to someone but I can't make out who. Then I hear his voice and I put all the pieces together. Brad's in jail.

Crap!

I filled my mug with coffee and stepped out onto the patio. The air is light this morning, and there is a chill that causes me to wrap my robe around myself even tighter. I opened up my missed calls and dialed the number from three thirty this morning. After only one ring, a lady picks up and my suspicions are confirmed.

After finding out about his bail and when he can be picked up, I headed back inside to find Ethan pouring himself coffee. I refilled my mug before saying anything. I'm sure he can tell that something is wrong. He hasn't said anything other than good morning and that's out of character for him. Maybe he's still upset about last night? I guess there's no better time to find out.

"So, I got a call from Brad last night. He's in jail." Unsure of how he might react to what I'm saying I avoid eye contact with him.

"Really? What the hell did he do?"

"They couldn't tell me why he was there, only that he could be picked up after nine and how much it was going to cost to get him out."

"Are you going to pick him up?"

I know that he already knew the answer to that. He was asking to see how I reacted. He was asking to validate a point that he was trying to make. He was asking because he wanted me to say no.

"If I don't then he'll have to sit there until someone else does."

"I'll go get him." His voice was strained. I could see the muscles in his shoulder tighten up, and I knew that he was doing it so that I wouldn't be alone with him. In a way, he was sacrificing his time to keep me away from Brad. He wanted to make sure that we weren't going to be alone together. This was his way of staking his claim.

"If you would rather that's fine." I can play this game too. I knew that he didn't want to go. "We could always go together if you want."

"No. I'll take care of it. I'm going to change and then I will head down there."

Without giving me a chance to answer, he's gone. This is not a good idea. If the two of them are alone together, there is no telling what will happen. I need to be in that car to run interference. Ethan doesn't give me that choice, however. I hear the garage door open and his car pulling out of the garage the second I shut the shower off. This is going to end badly and I am powerless to stop it.

Instead of waiting and worrying, I got ready and headed to campus early. I made my way to the cafeteria and picked up a coffee. After finding a spot on a couch, I rummaged through my bag, and pulled out everything for my next class. I was going to drown myself in school. Maybe it would take my mind off of what was going on.

An hour, and only two paragraphs later, I give up. I only have about twenty minutes before class starts, and I haven't comprehended anything that I have read, the little bit that it was. I pack my stuff back up and stand to leave. The hairs on the back of my neck stand up, and I can feel his presence before I can spot him in the crowd.

He looks like hell: two black eyes and a bandage around one wrist. He either gotten himself in a bar fight and I want to see the other guy, or he had gotten in a fight with Ethan and I don't want to see the other guy.

Crap!

I was hoping for the first option when I saw Ethan pop into view about ten feet behind him. There were no obvious marks on Ethan. The sight of him unscathed causes my heart to skip a beat, but I knew that with both of them walking towards me, that something was still going on. I sat back down on the couch and awaited their arrival.

They both stood in front of me waiting for me to say something but I was at a loss for words. They were towering over me, staring down at me, and I must have looked like a frightened child. I am terrified of what they might say, either one of them. I'm scared that Ethan left those marks on Brad's face. I'm worried that one or both of them might leave me. I can feel the butterflies fighting to break free. My heart is pounding. The sheer presence of the two of them and what they represent to me is just plain terrifying.

The look in Brad's eyes is one of disappointment, sorrow even. The look in Ethan's is one of anger, rage. It took me only mere moments to realize what had happened. Brad's left eye was freshly bruised and swollen. The right eye had been bruised long before the left.

"Becca," Ethan started. I could hear the anger he was trying to contain seep out in the way he said my name. "Brad has something that he needs to say."

I can see the hesitation on Brad's face. Ethan nudges him with his elbow in the ribs, and Brad winces like he's been hit with a baseball bat. He must have some bruising under his shirt. How badly was he beat? Who beat him that bad? Ethan?

"I would rather do this alone if you don't mind." He was directing his statement towards Ethan, not me, but he never stopped looking at me. I knew that Ethan didn't want to leave, but Brad was giving him no choice. In front of me, Ethan would always be a gentleman, and that meant granting Brad his request.

That's what he did, too. Right after kissing me deeply on the lips, and whispering his love in my ear. I knew he had said it loud enough for Brad to hear. He was, once again, finding a way to stake his claim on me. I was so confused that I didn't even know who to look at, so I watched as Ethan turned and walked out of the cafeteria. Even after he was through the doors and they had closed behind him, I was still staring.

I felt Brad sit down next to me, and when he took my hand, I let him. Whatever was going on was serious. He cleared his throat once, then twice, and tried to speak, but failed. I knew that he was trying to formulate the words, but he wasn't saying anything.

"What happened to you? You look like hell."

"Thanks. I've been better. I got a little drunk last night and got in a fight. The other guy looks worse than me. I would say that I won, but he didn't end up in jail and I did."

He was trying to make me smile or laugh or break the tension that was surrounding us but it wasn't working. "Seriously? Why? What the hell could have possessed you to get that drunk and start a fight?"

"First of all, I didn't start it. At least, I don't think I did. Secondly, I had just confessed my love to you, and when I got no response, I started to drink my problems away."

"Don't you dare blame this on me! What did you expect me to do? Did you expect me to leave Ethan? To run to you? To profess my love for you in a text?"

"No. I don't know what I expected, but I didn't expect the silence. It about killed me."

"Well, your text caught me completely off guard."

"Why did you let Ethan read it then?"

"What? I didn't. Why would I let him read it? That would break him. He would break you."

"He already tried. He took a cheap shot at me as soon as I was in the car. Caught me square in the eye." He was rubbing the eye that Ethan had punched him in.

"Well, I didn't let him read that text. He read the one before it, and the one that said to cancel your party, but he was in the shower when the last one came in, and I deleted it right away."

A long silence descended. I could hear the people around us chattering away, talking about their classes and gossiping about their friends. For a moment, it felt like I wasn't even there. It was like I was an outsider looking in. A fly on the wall of my own life. How had I let things go this far?

"I need to hear you say it, Becca."

I knew he was referring to his text. I knew he wanted me to tell him that I loved him. He wanted me to say the words out loud, to make them real. Did I? Was I?

I love him in the most unspoken kinds of ways. The way he holds my hand, like right now, because he knows that I need his support. The way he guides me with his hand on the small of my back. The way he looks at me with nothing but love and endearment all the time. I love the person that he is and the person that I am around him. I love his friendship and the way that friendship challenges me and has always challenged me.

"I don't know what to say. I do love you, Brad, more than you will ever know and more than I will ever understand. I also love Ethan, with all my heart and right now, he has my heart. He owns it, controls it, and protects it."

"Then I will wait. I'll wait for you, for your heart, for our chance to have more than just friendship. I'll wait for you but I can't wait forever. I've loved you for so long that I don't know how not to love you. When I figure it out is when I'll stop waiting. It probably won't be next week or even next month, but it will happen eventually. That's when I'll move on. Until then, I'll wait for you."

"Why? Why would you do that to yourself?"

"Because. As much as your heart belongs to Ethan, my heart belongs to you. It always has and pieces of it always will."

That's when I finally started to cry. I knew that I was going to be late for class. I knew that people were going to stare at the crazy girl on the couch crying. I knew that the conversations about class and the gossip about their friends would soon turn to curiosity about me and why I was crying. I just didn't care.

I cancelled Brad's party via text. When my phone started to go off nonstop with questions of why, I turned it off. I didn't want to explain why. I didn't really even know why. He had canceled his party, not me. He had decided to bring turmoil into our relationship, not me. Was I just an innocent bystander or was this my fault entirely?

I sent Brad a text saying *Happy Birthday* but I received no reply, not even a thank-you. The weekend came and went, and with finals week upon me, I was completely panicked. Ethan and I were speaking, but things were different. He wouldn't talk about what had happened with Brad, and neither would I. We were both smart enough to know not to push it.

I needed to talk to someone about all of it. My last conversation with Ella came to mind, and I just couldn't shake the feeling that now was the time to hear everything that she had to say. I knew that whatever it was that I was not going to like it, but that I probably needed to hear it. How bad could it be? It's not like it's my fault that they broke up…is it?

"Hey girl. What's going on?"

Her voice is refreshing. After all the drama that's been going on in my life it was nice to hear someone in a good mood for a change.

"Not much. Studying for finals."

"Oh. So this phone call has nothing to do with the fact that you and Brad are not speaking right now for reasons that I will refrain from rehashing."

Crap!

I'm not sure how she knows about all that when she lives so far away, but she does.

"Maybe a little."

"Figures. So, what happened?"

"Well, what have you heard already?"

"All I heard was that you broke his heart, he got in a fight, ended up in jail, got out, and then got in a fight with Ethan. But that was all before he canceled his birthday party. Are you two talking again yet?"

"Nope. I haven't seen or spoken to him since the day he got out of jail. I sent him a message on his birthday and he never replied."

"I'm sure he'll come around. He's just hurt, Becca. I knew that he wouldn't take the news of your engagement well."

"That's only part of it. We're also moving to England."

"Really? That's awesome. When?"

"After the holidays. Ethan starts his new job the first week of January."

"Oh. That quick, huh?"

"Yeah. I don't have a lot of time to get him to move past this."

"You don't have enough time in the world, Becca. He will never move past this, past you. You don't see that?"

"I do. That's the problem." I take a deep breath, knowing that once I ask her that she will tell me what I need to know, and that breathing may become a small problem. "Ella, I need to know why you guys broke up. You told me last time we talked that I should know."

"You should. I never wanted to be the one to tell you, but I have a feeling that Brad still isn't fully aware of why we broke up. Are you sure? Once I tell you this, you will never be able to erase it from your brain."

"Please. I need to know."

"Okay." There was a long pause before she continued. It was almost like she was mentally preparing herself to relive everything. As hard as this was going to be on me, I'm sure it is going to be harder on her. "The last few weeks that we were together were amazing. They were so different than the months before that. It was almost like our relationship was new again. That excitement was back. I was actually looking forward to seeing him every day, counting the hours or minutes until I was able to rush home to him. It was amazing. Then, two days before we broke up, I realized why things had changed."

I can hear the hurt in her voice. She truly loved Brad at one point in time, and he had broken her heart.

"You had practice every day that summer in the mornings. Ethan was working part-time at the country club in the afternoons, and you were working at that Mexican restaurant at night. I was working pretty much all day every day at the hotel, and Brad and I only got to see each other on his nights off. At first, I thought that because our time was limited that it became special. Then, that day I came home early because I wasn't feeling well, I realized what had changed. He had you all to himself every afternoon, all afternoon. It was just the two of you, hanging out. There was no one else but the two of you. It was like you guys were in your own world."

I remember that summer as clear as day. It was the summer after our freshman year. The summer right before Ethan and I moved in to a place of our own. Brad and I used to hang out and swim or play tennis or go exploring every afternoon that summer.

"That day I was sick, I walked in and found the two of you having a food fight in the kitchen. Do you have any idea what I really saw?"

"No." I could hear the uncertainty in my voice.

"I saw the love. I saw his love for you. It was clear as day. As much as I wanted to believe that he was in love with me, after seeing the two of you that day, I knew that he never had been. I knew that he would never love me, not like he loved you. I didn't want to have to compete for his love. It wouldn't have been a competition I could have won."

I'm shocked more than anything. Were his feelings for me that transparent back then? Was I the only person who had no idea what was going on?

"I'm so sorry, Ella. I had no idea."

"I know and I don't blame you. It was never your fault and it never will be. I don't even blame Brad anymore. I blame myself for falling in love with someone who I knew was never really available to begin with. He may have owned my heart once upon a time, but I never owned his. His heart has always belonged to you and only you, Becca."

I don't know what else to say to her. It all makes a little bit more sense now. Brad and Ella breaking up. Ethan wanting us to live alone. All of it. How is it that I was so blind to what was going on around me for so long. We lived together for a year.

∞

Graduation morning, I was surprised to find Ethan in the kitchen making breakfast for the two of us. He had brought home some packing boxes the day before, and it looked as though he had been up for a while. There were three boxes full in the living room waiting to be taped shut. It was a weird feeling, knowing that in less than a month that I would be on an entirely different continent.

I'm gazing off into space, thinking about all that's happening, about everything that Ella said, and all that's about to change. I can hear him talking in the background. I'm watching the coffee brew, focusing on each drip, knowing that I am that much closer to the start of another day.

I come to just as he sets our plates on the breakfast bar. We haven't eaten a single meal together since the ordeal with Brad last week. He worked late all week and I had been studying. Then finals were here, and all either of us did was study. We had both been avoiding each other, and doing a rather good job of it.

"So, how did your finals go?"

I was shoveling food in my face right as he asked me. I smiled and tried to quickly chew and swallow, but started to choke on my pancakes. He handed me my coffee and gently patted my back. The simple touch of his hand caused goose bumps to form on my arms, and a chill to run up my spine. Ethan noticed right away, and instead of waiting for me to answer his question, he scooped me up in his arms and carried me to our bedroom.

When we finally emerged, sweaty and tired, we reheated our pancakes and traded our coffee in for ice cold milk. As if nothing had happened, we sat back down at the bar and picked up where we had left off.

"Finals were fine. I know I passed, but I'm pretty sure that my lack of concentration was obvious in some of my work. I'll pass all my classes, but I won't be making straight As this semester. How do you think you did?"

"I don't care, really. They're giving me a diploma today no matter if I passed finals or not."

"Fair point. You still studied."

"I know. I couldn't go in there completely unprepared."

"So, you aced them then?" By the look on his face, I knew that his scores would beat mine any day. He couldn't do anything halfway, it just wasn't in his nature. "What time do we need to be at the auditorium today for the ceremony?"

"I have to be there by two and it starts at three, so you should probably just ride with me."

"Sounds like a plan. Are your parents going to be looking for me or should I try and find them?"

"Mom knows that you'll be sitting up front. You're going to have to save at least seven seats so that you all can sit together."

"Who else is coming? Your parents, my mom, and my sister."

Unglued

"Morgan and Natalie are coming, and Brad will be sitting with you guys too."

That got my attention. If my mouth had been full of food, I probably would have started to choke on it again. Why was Brad sitting with us? Why was he even going to the ceremony? If he wasn't answering my texts and he was avoiding me, why would he want to come to Ethan's graduation? I wanted to ask why, but instead, I just nodded and went back to eating my breakfast. Today was going to prove to be a very challenging day, I could feel it already.

Chapter Eight

Brad didn't show up for graduation. If he did, he didn't sit with us at least. I'm still not sure why Ethan invited him in the first place. It was completely out of character for him these days. I would have thought that he would want to keep Brad as far away from me as possible. Even without speaking about what happened, I knew that things had changed between us. The way he used to look at me was gone. The adoring stares that I used to see him giving me from time to time are now replaced with stares of curiosity.

Our relationship was on the fence and it was going to topple to one side or the other, soon. Which way it was going to fall was beyond me. Either way, I feel like I am going to be left in pieces. Either I was going to lose Ethan, or I was going to lose Brad. That was a simple fact that I needed to face.

We went to dinner as a family after the ceremony. Of course, everyone knew about our engagement, and that was the primary topic of conversation. Ethan had yet to tell his parents about his promotion, and with all the events that had been unfolding in the rest of our world, I had yet to tell my mother. I hadn't even mentioned Brad's stint in jail to her. His absence today caused her to ask questions. I didn't have any answers for her, and I could see the big red flag flying high as I shrugged my shoulder, trying to be as nonchalant as possible.

"So, I have an announcement to make." Ethan's voice brought me back to the reality before me. He was about to announce our move, and the thought scared me half to death. Either my mother was going to be incredibly happy for us, or incredibly mad at me for not telling her. I was about to find out.

"I have been offered a huge promotion and I, we," he said, motioning in my direction, "have decided that I should accept it."

Applause from our families was louder than usual. I could feel everyone in the restaurant staring at our table. It didn't help matters that Ethan was standing, towering over our table with his glass raised high.

"Becca and I will be moving to England in a couple of week where I will be running the newest gallery for Art Wave."

The applause he had received from our friends and families was silenced in an instant. The looks of shock on their faces were more than I could take. I could feel my mother's stare on me as I focused on my clenched hands in my lap. This was supposed to be a good thing for us, but I was getting a really bad vibe from everyone else at the table. We should have talked to them about it. It was a huge decision. We should have included them.

"What about school? Are you planning on going to school over there or are you dropping out?" My mother's voice was full of concern and anger and disbelief. This was not the way I wanted her to find out. Ethan should have known that. I should have stopped him from making the announcement.

"I applied for a study abroad program. I should hear back before Christmas. If I'm accepted, then I will be studying over there. If not, I plan to defer a semester and come back for summer classes. Maybe."

No one else at the table had said anything yet. I needed someone to voice their opinion. I needed someone to say something to break the silence that had enveloped our table. I needed to get away from this. My breathing was rapid and I could feel a panic attack coming on. Ethan gently squeezed my shoulder, knowing that something was wrong, but I couldn't look at him, or anyone else. I kept staring at my hands, clenched so tightly together that I thought for a moment that I was going to lose feeling in my fingertips.

That's when I bolted.

The bathroom at the restaurant was actually pretty nice. There were a few shreds of toilet paper on the floor, but the stall walls were lacking in the gossip department, something that's hard to find at most restaurants within a few miles of campus.

I stood with my back to the door, hands on my knees, and my head down, until it felt like the world was no longer spinning around me. My gut was telling me that I was making a huge mistake, but I wasn't sure if that was because of the way my mom had looked at me, or because I was really making a mistake.

Knowing that I was going to have her support no matter what didn't ease the nausea. The simple fact that I had put off telling my mother, unconsciously or not, was a key indicator that things weren't right. The night we had decided to go, I had felt no reservations about the decision. I hadn't felt much of anything about the decision. I wasn't overly excited or overly scared. I wasn't anxious. I wasn't thinking about packing.

I was indifferent. I made the decision to go based on the fact that I felt like I would hold Ethan back if I didn't say yes. The pieces were starting to fall together, and the fact that I was making a mistake was coming to light. I stood up straight and with new resolve. I was going to tell Ethan that I didn't want to go, that I was having some reservations, and that maybe he should go ahead without me and that I would come over on break.

He would be okay with that. Right? He wouldn't not go because I was staying behind. Right? This was as close to a dream job as he was going to get. A once in a lifetime opportunity. He wouldn't turn this down.

I heard the bathroom door open and then softly close. I heard the lock click into place and wondered why someone felt the need to lock the door behind them. Did they know I was in here? Maybe I should climb on top of the seat and wait them out. Have they seen my feet yet? I was standing by the door so they couldn't have missed them.

"You can come out here or stay in there, but I think we need to talk."

Why was he here? Did he really think that it was a good idea to lock us in the bathroom together? I had already spent enough time in a women's bathroom with him. I didn't need a repeat performance.

Knowing that he wouldn't leave until I came out, I unlatched the stall door. He was leaning against the counter, dressed to the nines in what looked like a three-piece suit minus the jacket. His tie was already loosened, and I knew that he had probably had a drink, or two. His black eyes were healing; the right one was barely bruised now.

"So, your mom looks a little upset, and you're hiding in the bathroom. What happened?"

"Ethan announced his promotion and our move. I hadn't had a chance to tell her yet."

"Hadn't had a chance to tell her or didn't tell her? There's a big difference."

He was right. I talked to my mom practically every day. If I wasn't able to find the time to call her, I would send her a text. The only other people in my life that I was that close to were Brad, Ethan, Natalie, and Ella. Lainey and Jill had both moved to Phoenix after our first year of college, and I rarely hear from them anymore.

"I didn't know how to tell her, I guess. I knew that she would be upset that I was leaving but I also knew that the fact that I was probably not going to go to school over there would make her even more upset." I didn't want her to think that I was following Ethan and letting my dreams go. I wasn't doing that. Was I?

"Don't go then."

"It's not that simple and you know it. Ethan only accepted the promotion because I told him that I would go with him. He wasn't even going to mention it to me because he thought that he would lose me if he left without me. He was sure that I wouldn't want to go."

"So, what changed your mind? Why did you say yes?"

"I don't know."

"I do." The smile on his face said it all. The glisten in his eyes told me that he wasn't going to share.

"Care to tell me? I'm pretty sure that you weren't there when…" *Crap!* He was there, sort of. He was on the other end of the line, texting me. I was upset with him that night. He was confusing me. Ethan called and told him we were moving that night.

"I don't need to tell you what you already know. I may not have physically been there, but I was there. I will always be there." It was like he was telling me everything that I needed to hear. I needed to know that he would always be there for me, no matter what. I needed to hear him say it, to make it real.

I was so lost in what he was saying that I didn't realize that he was now standing in front of me. He was holding my hand and softly caressing my knuckles with his thumb. He was making his play for me.

That's when it hit me. Leaving here was more about leaving him than it was about anything else. If I left with Ethan, I was letting go of Brad. If I moved away then I was putting space between us. It would be over, for good, no going back, no changing my mind. Over.

When he kissed me, my mind went blank and my body took over. I knew in that moment that what I was doing was wrong. I knew that I was going to have to tell Ethan, and that he was going to be upset, angry, broken.

The moment I started to return his kiss was when I realized that I wasn't going to be able to leave him. The last time I left, it wasn't my choice. This time would be different.

When Brad finally released me, I took an immediate step back as if I had been burned. My body was on fire, my heart was aching, and I knew that if he kissed me like that again, if I allowed him to, then there would be no turning back. I wasn't ready for this. I needed time to think, to analyze the situation.

"I have to get back to dinner." That was the best I could come up with.

I knew that I didn't need an excuse to leave the bathroom. I knew that he would have let me walk out without saying anything. I needed to remind myself, in that moment, that there was someone else waiting for me.

I didn't look back as I unlocked the door and stepped out into the hallway. My mom was waiting for me with a knowing look on her face. Had she seen Brad go into the bathroom? Had anyone seen him?

"So, did you change your mind in there?" She had definitely seen him go into the bathroom. "I was going to try and eavesdrop on your conversation but I thought waiting here was more appropriate. Ethan thinks that I went after you. He thinks that you and I are having a moment in the bathroom. What do you suppose I tell him we talked about?"

"You don't have to cover for me. I need to talk to him. I need to tell him what's going on before he finds out from someone else."

"What exactly is going on, Becca?"

"Well, for starters, I need to tell him how I feel about Brad. If he'll still have me after he hears that, then I'll let you know what's going on. If not..."

I let my voice trail off, trying not to think about what would happen if Ethan decided not to forgive me. I knew there was a chance. I knew

Unglued

that my life would drastically change. I knew all these things before I let Brad kiss me, yet I'm still somehow in this situation. Again.

"Well, I hope he understands. You two have a long history, one that started before Ethan was even in the picture. If he can't understand, then it's his loss."

"Thanks, Mom." I gave her a quick hug and as I'm about to pull away, I can hear Ethan's voice traveling through the restaurant. A small shiver races through my body. His voice is smooth and loving. He doesn't sound the least concerned with my whereabouts. "So, how about we finish dinner?"

"Sounds good. They took our plates back to the kitchen to keep them warm. You've, we've, been gone for a while."

"I know. I need to get back to my fiancé." In more ways than one, I suppose.

As we were walking back to the table, I see Brad sneak out the front door of the restaurant. I wouldn't have recognized him if I hadn't known what he was wearing. He had somehow found a hat and a pair of glasses to complete his outfit.

After dinner was through, and Ethan and I were on our way home, is when I finally started to realize that this was going to be a very defining moment in our relationship. This was going to be hard for me to say and probably even harder for him to hear. If we could work through this though, we could work through anything. If we could move on, both of us, from my past, then we could start to build our future together.

Ethan was tired and went straight to the shower. It gave me time to think about what I was going to say and even more time to worry about how I was going to say it. He needed to know the truth, all of it. He needed to know about every stolen kiss. He needed to know about every heartfelt sentiment. Above all else, he needed to know how I felt.

I was sitting in the middle of our bed, Indian-style, when he emerged from the bathroom. He gave me a quick smile and disrobed in front of me. His gorgeous body was completely distracting me from my current thoughts. I watched as he pulled out a pair of underwear and slowly put them on. I watched as he rummaged around in his drawers for a pair of gym shorts and a t-shirt. The way his muscles danced as he moved. The way his tattoo stretched when he reached farther into the drawer. Finally, as he turned around, the way his hips sat just beautifully above the waistband of his shorts. I was entranced by him, by his body, and I felt my own body starting to react.

He knew what he was doing. Consciously, not subconsciously. He was aware that he was driving me crazy, and he was doing it to prove a point. What point he was trying to prove is beyond me, but I didn't really care anyway. He was good at getting reactions out of me in the most interesting ways.

"So, what happened at dinner tonight?" And all of the sudden I was no longer interested in anything. My body immediately froze up, and my stomach dropped like a rock sinking to the bottom of a lake.

"What do you mean? I felt faint, so I went to the bathroom to put some water on my face." Good lie, Becca. Believable. Somewhat the truth but not entirely. He would have to believe me. Right?

"I know you a little better than that. Plus, your mom looked shocked. Why didn't you just tell her?"

Crap!

He wasn't going to believe me now. Anything I had planned to say was going to be based on my first crappy lie. I was going to have to try the truth.

"I don't know. I think I was scared."

"That makes sense, but you shouldn't be scared. You're an adult and can make decisions that other people don't have to like. It's your life, remember?"

Great segway. Thank you, Ethan, for leading me onto my next topic that I really don't want to discuss with you. Now or never. I'm not going to get another opportunity like this, and I have to take advantage of it.

"So, about that."

The smile on his face just fell. I can see that he's been blinded by my simple statement. I haven't even broken any news to him and yet he already knows that he's not going to like it.

"I've been thinking about England, and I'm just not as sure as I used to be."

"What's this about, Becca? You were sure the other day and now you are having second thoughts? What changed your mind? Who changed your mind?"

When he said who, I about lost it. I could already feel the tears welling up knowing that I have, in a way, disappointed him. I've broken an unspoken promise to him. We may not have taken our vows yet, but I knew that kissing Brad was wrong, yet I did it anyway. This was not about England. This was about my insecurities. This was about me.

"It has nothing to do with anything but me not being sure that I want to go. Maybe you should go, and I can come over and visit, and if things are going well for you over there, then I will consider moving."

"The point of going was to go together. I didn't want to go without you. You knew this, and yet you convinced me to take the job. Did you plan on backing out the whole time?"

"What? No! I'm just not sure any more."

"Why?"

"I don't know!"

"I think you do. Tell me, Becca. Tell me!"

He's yelling. I've never heard him yell before, at least not at me. I feel the anger and frustration radiating from his body, and it's more than I can take. Before I even realize what I'm doing, I start talking, telling him everything that I wish I didn't have to.

"I kissed Brad! Is that what you want to hear? I kissed him and I'm falling apart on the inside. I love you so much and I don't know why I kissed him, but I did. I want us to be together, but I'm not sure I'm ready to leave him behind. I love him too!"

That was the last of our conversation. I don't know exactly what happened after he left the house, but I remember him leaving. I remember lying awake that night and crying. I remember wishing that I had never told him. I remember wishing that I had been stronger. Strong enough to stop things from happening with Brad. Strong enough to leave and move to England with Ethan. Strong enough to resist the pull that Brad has on my heart.

Now, I wish I had been strong enough to hold myself together that night. I wish I had been strong enough to hold myself together the next day, the next week, and the next month. I wasn't strong, however. I was weak, and grew weaker by the moment when I realized that Ethan wasn't coming back.

I moved my stuff the last week of December. I knew he wasn't expecting me to be there since I had been staying at my mom's. I was just putting the last load in my trunk when he pulled in the driveway. I could see that he was surprised. I could also see that he was deciding whether or not to turn around and leave.

Instead of giving him the upper hand and allowing him to make the decision, I made it for him. I dropped the box in my trunk and drove away without looking back. I knew that I was acting cold, but in actuality, it was the only way that I could mask the sadness that I didn't want him to see. The pain that I was trying to hide from everyone around me, including myself. The pain that was evident no matter how hard I tried.

The only thing of mine that was left in that house was my heart. I left it in a note that was under the engagement ring he had given me on the kitchen counter. I knew that he would find it, and I knew that he would read it. I also knew that things between us were over. According to his mother, he was on a flight to England the next day.

Chapter Nine

It's been two months since Ethan left for England, and I haven't heard a word from him. I didn't really expect to hear from him at all in the beginning. That was until last week when I heard my mom on the phone with him. She was telling him how miserable I was. She was giving him details on how I hadn't left the house in weeks. She was telling him things that he didn't need to hear. Whose side was she supposed to be on?

It was in that moment that I vowed to get back on my feet. The first thing I did was call Natalie. She had tried to stop over a number of times when I was refusing all visitors. I owed her an apology, and an explanation. I was unfair to all of my friends. They were there for me, in person or via text. They all tried to call. Some tried harder than others, but in the end, I treated them all the same—poorly. I was in a dark place and no one was going to be able to break the walls I had built except Ethan himself and, in a way, I guess he did.

The last thing on Natalie's mind was me turning her away. She understood better than I thought she would. I was broken by love. I had always thought that love was something that would build you up, make you happy. I never imagined the crushing impact love could have on someone. The pain and hurt that it leaves in its wake after it's gone.

The fact that I was now fully aware of those things made me skeptical that I ever wanted to fall in love again. I fell apart the day that Ethan left me. I felt it when my heart started to crack into pieces. I thought about the joy and happiness that we had shared. The pain of those incredible memories caused me to break down and cry when I realized that I had thrown it all away. I had caused my own heart to shatter the day I put it all in perspective and realized that, in the end, it was all my fault.

Natalie and I met for coffee twice that first week, and talked about nothing important and everything unimportant. She knew that I was still fragile, and that it would take time for me to heal. On the outside, I tried to appear as normal as possible. On the inside, there was still a storm raging. Every time it tried to show itself, I did my best to swallow it whole. I would push it down as deep as possible. After a few weeks it became easier, but I knew that it was just a matter of time before it would reappear and bring with it new turmoil. The question became when, not if, it would reappear.

Once our coffee dates started to become a more regular thing, she started to invite some of our other friends along. She was slowly re-introducing me to society. I had deferred a semester, and been out of the loop for so long, that I didn't really know what to talk to my friends about. Most of the time, I just sat back and listened. Every so often, one of them would ask my opinion on something and I would give it with as much confidence as I could muster.

It wasn't until weeks later that I realized that I was the one initializing the conversations. I was the one who wanted to talk about the things that I was missing out on. Mostly, we talked about classes. Every so often, we would talk about a new movie coming out, or the latest episode of our favorite shows on television. No one ever mentioned a boyfriend and Natalie never brought up Morgan or their wedding plans.

I knew that they all thought that they were helping me. I also knew that the only way I was going to completely heal, at least as much as I was ever going to heal, was to talk about the things that I wanted to avoid talking about most. I wasn't ready to breach topics like Natalie and Morgan's wedding, but I was ready to talk about tennis. I was ready to face those demons.

"So, how is the tennis team this year?" The looks of surprise on the faces of my friends range from the standard "oh my god" to Natalie's smug smile, that told me she knew what I was doing. "Has anyone beat Heather yet?"

Stunned silence was not the reaction that I had thought I would receive, but it's what I got. No one was quite sure how to answer my questions, or even if they wanted to. They were still looking a gasp and confused when I excused myself to the restroom. I knew that Natalie would crack their heads together while I was gone.

When I returned, it was like it had never even happened. We talked about tennis for the next few weeks. Kelly gave me the play-by-play of what the team was doing, and gave me the breakdown of how my archrival was playing this year. I wasn't ready to face her yet. She knew that she was responsible, in a small way at least, for my injury. She was coming into town to play in a few weeks. I wanted to go watch the team play. I wanted to face her. I knew I wouldn't be able to do it alone, and that's when I allowed my thoughts to drift to Brad for the first time since putting myself on house arrest.

He hadn't come by the house since the first week I was home. I had asked him to stay away. I thought that if I distanced myself far enough from him that maybe, just maybe, Ethan would come back to me. That Ethan would forgive me and call and ask me to come to England. I really thought that if I gave Brad up, for good this time, that Ethan and I would work things out. I had thought wrong.

"Becca?"

"Yeah? What's up? What did I miss?" I hadn't realized that I had zoned out. I'm not sure how long I had been in my own little world, but all of my friends were staring at me. No, they weren't staring at me, they were staring past me. As soon as I realized that, I also realized that I had goose bumps and that my body was tingling.

He was here. My body hadn't reacted like this since the night Ethan left me. I remember the sensations that had coursed through my body as I had watched him disrobe and then dress. I can still smell the body wash that he had used that night. Why can I smell the body wash that he used that night?

Natalie's face was telling me a story that I didn't want to know. The uncertainty was apparent. I knew that there was no avoiding what was about to happen. I was going to have to face him. I was going to have to deal with this head on. There was no sneaking out the back and avoiding him. He was obviously here. He had obviously seen me. And judging by the apologetic expression that Natalie just gave me, he was walking in this direction.

The storm that had been raging inside me for so long started to calm. I would have thought that now would be that moment where it would try to break free. The moment I realized who was standing behind me is the moment I knew why the storm wasn't raging.

His scent surrounded me, and when his strong hand touched my shoulder, I jumped a little. My friends began to pack up their belongings and excuse themselves one by one, except Natalie. She grabbed onto my hand and looked straight into my eyes for confirmation. I gave her a nod of approval before she let go and left me alone with him.

"You look amazing."

He was sitting next to me now, just close enough that I could reach out and touch his face if I wanted to. I think I only did it to make sure that he was real. To make sure that I wasn't imagining him since I had just been thinking about him. To make sure my mind wasn't playing another trick on me. I hadn't seen him in almost three months, and those three months had been good to him. He looked as handsome as ever and my heart started to ache.

"Thanks. You look good, too."

"Can I buy you a coffee?" What a loaded question. It came out sounding simple, but what I really heard was *can I please spend time with you?*

"I have one, but, thanks. What are you doing here?"

"I was passing by and I saw you in the window. I had to stop."

"How did you even know it was me?"

"I don't need to see your face to know it's you, Becca. I would be able to pick you out of a crowd from any angle. I see your face every time I close my eyes, and you are all I dream about. I told you that I would wait for you, for our time."

"Brad, I just…" What do I say to that? He loves me still, after all this time. After choosing Ethan over him, after the way I treated him after Ethan left, after everything that we've been through, he still loves me.

How is that possible? I had been so terrible to him. I had turned him away. I had blamed him. I shut him out of my life without so much as an explanation. He knew what I was thinking but he didn't really know why. He didn't know what I had told Ethan that night. He didn't know that I had confessed to loving him.

"I know that things are still confusing for you. I know that you still need time to heal, time to grieve, time to understand it all."

He was right. I still needed time to understand it all. That was the biggest part of all this. How had I let everything go so far?

It hurt. That pain in my chest was back, and it hurt. Just looking at him, the unmistakable look of sorrow on his face, the twinkle of hope in his eyes, was too much. This was all too much for me to handle right now. It felt like the walls were closing in on me. It was almost as if his love for me was suffocating me at that moment.

"I do. I need more time."

I pulled my hand away from his and placed it gently in my lap, afraid that the smallest movement will give away the effect that he's having on me right now. The uncertainty that I feel. I pulled my emotions back and the storm begins to stir.

The slight shift in his demeanor told me that he understood what I was asking him. He knew that I needed him to leave. That I needed him to give me time, and that I meant time alone, without him around to influence my decision.

He stood slowly and smiled. He gave me a quick kiss on the forehead and was gone as quickly as he had arrived. I knew that my friends were lurking somewhere, but I couldn't see them. Natalie was the only one to come back to the table. She sat quietly while my mind processed what had just happened. She was waiting.

I felt the tears begin to fall. I had not allowed myself to cry in what felt like forever. I had been putting on such a big front for all of my friends, for my mom, for me, that I had not allowed myself to feel any type of emotion.

"He still loves me." It was all I could say. It was really the only thing that was important to me at that moment. It was the only thing that my brain had processed. It's like my mind was stuck on repeat. I wanted to replay our entire conversation over again in my head, but the only thing my brain wanted to comprehend was that one little, incredibly important fact.

"I know. I can't believe that you would ever doubt that."

She knew? How is that possible? She must have seen the wheels turning, or the expression I gave was one of shock, because when she continued, she explained everything.

"He called me the night of graduation. He knew that he had broken you. He knew that what he had said to you was wrong, and that you would end up telling Ethan. He knew that it wouldn't turn out well, and he felt terrible. Morgan invited him over and we all sat around and tried to figure out how he was going to fix it. By the next morning, we knew that it wasn't possible. That's when he broke. I have never seen him cry. He knew he had caused you pain and that there was no way for him to fix it, and he broke down. After the holidays, when you turned him away is when he really broke. He was on autopilot every day. He would go to school, go to work, and go home. He never went out anywhere. He never called anyone. Morgan called him a couple times a week to see how he was doing, but he only answered half the time. We finally got him out of the house after a couple months and got him to go out with us one night. It was a struggle the entire time we were out. He was drunk after a few hours, and by the time we dropped him off at his place, he was babbling about you. How much he loves you. How bad he screwed up. How sorry he was for even moving here. I didn't know who to call to help him. He was just as broken as you were."

Holy Crap!

I had no idea that my relationship had broken him too. He was not responsible for our breakup. I played as big of a part, if not bigger, than he did. I was the one who chose to act the way I did. I was the one who needed to claim responsibility. I was the one who was in love with two people. He just loved me.

"What happened after that? He seems fine now." I'm sure she could hear the hesitation in my voice as I asked.

"He's better. It took a minute to figure out what he needed, but I finally did. I called Ethan."

"*You what*? Why would you do that?" I screamed out of pure shock. How could she do that?

"It actually helped him. They talked for about an hour. They yelled and screamed and then calmed down and talked it out. I don't know exactly what was said, but whatever it was, it helped. He's been his normal self for the past month or so. I have to say, it's nice to have him back. You too."

I hadn't realized it, but I had not only broken up with Ethan, or rather he broke up with me, but I had broken up with Brad too. I had broken our friendship. I had broken all ties with him to try and save my relationship with Ethan. It hadn't helped at all. It had been a pointless gesture to end our friendship, to try and save something that had already been lost. Ethan was still gone and apparently, he was talking to everyone but me now.

Thank goodness for Natalie. She was the one thing that was holding me together. She was the one person who truly understood what I was going through, what we were all going through. I had no idea until that moment that she was the glue that was holding us all together through this entire mess. Without her, I have no idea where I would be right now.

I needed to talk to Brad. I needed to know what Ethan said to help him get his life back. I wanted my life back. I wanted to be normal again, or as normal as I ever was. I wanted to feel like I was living with a purpose. I wanted to stop feeling like everyone was watching and waiting for me to break again. I wanted to be the strong person that I used to be. More than anything, I wanted to find a way to forgive myself for the things that I had done so that I could move on.

"Thanks Natalie. I think I finally know what I need to do."

Chapter Ten

I was looking up at one of the most beautiful three-story building I had ever seen. The architecture was magnificent. The brick, although probably very old, was in great condition, and gave the building an incredibly rustic feel. The large windows look like they were a newer addition to the building. They looked great, but they took something away from the building. I knew that the building was probably a hundred years old. The windows, the modern design of them, must have come from a remodel in the last few years.

It was hard to believe that it was a hotel. I was so impressed with what it looked like on the outside that I was imagining a million different ways it would look on the inside. The only way to find out was to check in to my room. As I stepped through the revolving door, I was not disappointed.

The lobby was very modern contemporary. Everything was white and black and red. Every wall was a pristine white. The couches were red leather, and none of them had arm rests. All of the tables were black wrought iron with glass tops. The artwork revolved around the color scheme as well. It's like the painting were made specifically to fit in here. They were either black and white or black and white with vivid red to make them stand out more.

My room was the same as the lobby. The walls and bedding were both white. The furniture was black wood or wrought iron. The artwork all had splashes of red. Every lamp or clock or little embellishment to the room was red. It was amazing how great they could make a room look, even one as small as this one, using just three colors.

Once I stepped into the bathroom is when the color scheme fell apart for me. The bathroom was black and white, but the tiles in the shower were red. It didn't have the same appeal as the rest of the hotel. Had they used a red shower curtain and black tiles, it would have been better. Who was I to judge, though? I was just visiting.

I quickly unpacked a few things, took a few moments to make my hair look good and my make-up look fresh, then headed back down to the lobby. I stopped at the desk and asked the clerk for a map and directions. Once I thought I knew where I was going, I set off on foot. I could have easily taken a cab, but I knew that I would enjoy the walk more. It gave me time to think, time to figure out exactly what I was going to say. I had flown across the

Atlantic to see him. I didn't want to screw it up now.

London is a beautiful city. So beautiful, in fact, that while I was enjoying the sights, I eventually got lost. The gallery had a show tonight at six and I wanted to make sure that I was there. It was Ethan's first show. From what Natalie had said, the gallery had successfully put on three or four shows for local artists since Ethan had arrived. Tonight it was his turn. He was going to be showing his work for everyone to see.

I found a café and stopped in. I grabbed a coffee and asked them to call me a cab. The lady behind the counter didn't seem overly enthusiastic to be helping me, but did so anyway. I sat at a table by the front window and waited for the cab to arrive. It was close to six and I wanted to make sure that I made it on time. The lady had said that I was only about six blocks from the gallery, but my feet hurt, and I didn't want to walk anymore.

When it pulled up, I ran outside to flag him down. I hopped in and told him where I needed to go. He pulled away from the curb and sped towards the gallery without saying a word. The back of the cab was different than I would have imagined. It wasn't your standard yellow on the outside either. Everything was a bit different in London.

Pulling up outside of the gallery was when my nerves went on high alert. I knew that he was in there. I knew that the second I walked into the room, that he would know I was there. I knew that he would either run from me and I would ruin his night, or he would run to me. Either way, things were about to change.

I think the thought of actually talking to him scared me the most. I hadn't quite worked out what I was going to say. I wasn't quite sure of how I wanted to approach him. There was obviously no other reason for me to come to England. He was the only person I knew here. He was the only reason I would come here. I was supposed to have come here with him three months ago.

Natalie and I discussed my trip just yesterday as I packed. She was giving me her standard "confidence boosting" pep talk, or at least she was trying. I was only half listening to her until she said his name. Ethan. That's all it took to get my attention.

I listened to her tell me all about what he's doing right now. I listened to her tell me about the success he's had since coming here. The fact that he was having a show of his own was a testament to how hard he was working.

I had wanted to bounce ideas off of her. I wanted to hear how she thought that he would react to seeing me. I wanted to know if he ever asked about me, about how I was doing. The words just wouldn't come out. All I did was listen. I was too afraid to engage in the conversation.

The large front windows gave me a nice view into the front room of the gallery. I recognized some of Ethan's artwork, but not all of it. I decided that it's now or never. I asked the cabbie to come back and get me in an hour and he agreed. I paid the cabbie and thanked him before getting out, but I only got a muffled response.

His name is on a large banner that's hanging from the ceiling as soon as you walk through the front doors. His artwork is surrounding me, and for the first time, I am actually scared to see him. I am scared to be surrounded by all of Ethan's emotions. I can feel everything in that moment. I can feel his pain, his anguish, his hatred, and his love. So many emotions in one room that I have to step back outside and catch my breath.

That's when I see him. As he walks into the front room, the first thing I notice is the woman on his arm. She's beautiful and he's smiling. I can't see his dimple, but his smile seems sincere.

I can tell that she is guiding him, but I don't see him putting up much of a fight. She's gliding through the room, pointing from photograph to photograph. He's smiling and nodding but not saying much. If I didn't know better, I would think that she was trying to sell him a piece of artwork.

    This could be my only chance. I need to go to him and say all the things that I've been trying to find a way to say. I need to open my heart and tell him how I feel. I need to do something besides stand here and stare. I need to do something now.

    I run. I run before he can see me standing in the entrance, before he realizes that I'm here. The feelings that I'm getting are so overwhelming. The most eager to break free is jealousy. Ethan may not be mine anymore, but I do not like seeing another woman touching him, holding him, close to him at all. Jealousy is raging inside of me, and the fresh air is doing nothing to soothe it.

    I turn around and stare at him through the safety of the window. It's dark outside. There was no way he would be able to see me, but I can see him and everything that's going on around him. What I really need to do is keep running but I can't. My feet feel like they have cement blocks around them now. My heart is beating like crazy in my chest. My breathing is rapid and my breaths are shallow. My emotions are bubbling at the surface and trying to break free. I can feel the strength I have been looking for over the past few month break the surface, and just as I'm about to take my first step back towards the gallery, I freeze with my foot midair.

    They're bringing a new piece into the room and the sight of it makes my breath catch in my throat. I'm pretty sure I gasp, but no one is around to hear me. The smile is gone from Ethan's face as they place the photograph in its reserved space on the wall. I can see him say something to the woman, but she just shakes her head. He bends down and whispers something in her ear, and when she shakes her head again, he walks away from her and disappears through a door.

    I want to go after him but the photograph draws me in again. It's the most beautiful thing I have ever seen. The focus is distorted and the shading is perfect. Ethan always had a good knack for knowing when to try something new, even if it's on an old photograph. The gallery lighting is spotlighting the portrait perfectly, and before I know it, I'm standing right in front of it.

    No one is around me, thankfully. It's a weird feeling, staring at yourself. I can see the love in my eyes. I can feel it in my heart. I remember the day he took the photo. I was standing in our backyard. We weren't doing anything special that day. Ethan had just gotten his new camera, and had wanted to shoot some pictures just to get the feel of it. I was his favorite subject. At least, that what he used to say.

Out of the corner of my eye, I see a group of people approaching, and I back away and turn towards another photograph. I don't want to be recognized. All of the sudden, I don't want him to know that I'm here. I need to leave the gallery. I need to leave London. It hasn't been long enough. The look of pain in his eyes when they brought out the photograph was unmistakable. He was still grieving. He was still hurt.

Looking up, I realize that this photograph is of me too. Once I start to look around, I can see that there are quite a few of me. I can see that he's chosen different sides of my personality to display. There are a few of me smiling. There is one of me playfully frowning. There is even one of me playing tennis. The one that really makes me sad is the one of me he must have taken when I wasn't paying attention.

You can clearly see that I am lost in thought. It's not a close up of my face like some of the others. You can see most of my body. My eye is drawn to my hands. You can see my engagement ring, and you can see that I was probably twisting it on my finger. I'm standing in our kitchen, probably waiting for the coffee pot to finish brewing. I have his sweatshirt on and, if I remember right, he must have taken this the morning of his graduation.

I can feel the tears streaming down my face. There's no stopping them at this point. He's ripped my heart out with one photograph. I reach out and touch it and remember that everything is for sale. I quickly pull my hand back. I have to have it. If not just to remind myself of what I've done on a daily basis, but also so he doesn't have to be reminded of it. So maybe, just maybe, he can heal.

I quickly locate the man who is taking care of the sales. I try not to make eye contact, knowing he will recognize me if I do, and I give him a false name and address to ship it to. Natalie will understand when it arrives. I pay by credit card, not realizing that my real name is on my card until I'm signing the receipt. I wonder if he even looked.

After everything is situated, I rush to the front door to escape. It hasn't been quite an hour yet but the cabbie is sitting out front waiting for me. I take one last look into the gallery as I open the door. I can clearly see more photographs of me. I watch as the man puts a sold sign on the one I've just purchased, and I take one last look at Ethan as he comes back out the door he went through earlier.

Unglued

He walks over to the photograph that I purchased and gives it a long hard look before shaking his head and walking away. He captured on film the moment it all started to fall apart. The moment I went weak and started to question our relationship. He captured so much in that one photograph. He captured my fear and my weakness. My indecision. He captured the end of everything, and he may not have even known it at the time.

I'm standing with the cab door open when he approaches the window and looks out, directly to where I'm standing. I know that he can't see out the window, that he's probably staring at his own reflection, but it feels like he's staring into my soul. My heart skips a few beats and my pulse speeds up again. I know that I should go back in, say something to him, anything, but I can't bring myself to move.

I can see his lips move. I know that he's saying something, but I can't hear him through the glass. Is he talking to me? As the thought crosses my mind, I see the same woman as before appear from behind him and put her hand on his shoulder. She's saying something and before I realize what's happening, she's leading them back into the sea of people in the gallery, and they disappear amongst the crowd.

When the cab pulls up to the hotel, I pay the driver and get out without saying anything this time. I feel numb on the inside. I feel like I've been gutted. I know that I brought all this on myself. I know that everything that happened is all my fault. I know that there is no fixing what I broke and that this trip was my eye opener to it all. I know it's time to move on.

Chapter Eleven

I left England only one day after arriving. I was supposed to be there for an entire week. The week was supposed to be full of happy memories that Ethan and I would create. It was supposed to be full of us doing touristy things, and rekindling our relationship. I was supposed to leave there with a sense of purpose, with a sense of accomplishment. I was supposed to leave there feeling like everything was going to be just fine. I was supposed to fix things.

By the time I arrived home, all I felt was emptiness. I could feel my heart beating in my chest. The sound it was producing was overwhelming. I knew that I was broken, but still my heart continued to beat on, through the pain and tears. Through the sadness that overwhelmed my body. My heart beat on, louder and louder, the closer my plane came to landing back in Tucson.

Walking through the terminal felt like it took me forever. By the time I finally reached the baggage claim and spotted Natalie, it felt like I had been gone the week that I was supposed to have been.

I could see the sorrow in her eyes. She had been the one I called when I got back to the room. She had been the one to make the changes to my flight plan for me. She had been the one that told me over and over again that everything would be okay. The look in her eyes was betraying her. Everything was not going to be okay.

Unglued

She tried her best to perk me up. She kept me talking about the sights that I did see. She asked me about my hotel room over and over again. I described everything to her, but the only thing I could see perfectly clear in my mind was the hollow look in Ethan's eyes, when they hung the portrait of me on the wall. The shell of the person that he had become. The person that I had created.

I didn't tell her about the portrait that was being shipped to her house. The man I had paid told me that it would be six to eight weeks before I would see it, maybe longer. It was to remain hung in the gallery until Ethan's show was complete in two weeks, and then it would be carefully packaged and sent to the States.

It didn't really matter. I had no intention of unwrapping it when it arrived. I had no intention of hanging in on the wall of my bedroom, or anywhere else for that matter. I planned on sticking it in my closet, and keeping it as a constant reminder of what I had done. I didn't have to open it to know what it looked like. The look on my face was engrained so deep in my brain that I would never be able to forget it.

I hadn't called my mom to tell her that I was coming home early, so when I walked in the house, she was surprised to say the least. I knew that she wanted to ask about my trip, but I didn't give her the opportunity. I dropped my luggage in the hall, and headed to my room. I didn't have the strength to relive what had happened yet. I didn't know if I ever would.

I flopped down on my bed, and curled up in the fetal position. I had cried until my eyes hurt when I was in England. I had no tears left at this point, but that didn't keep my body from convulsing as if I were.

When I woke up the next morning, I wasn't alone. I knew that it was only a matter of time before he showed up, but I didn't realize that it would be this soon. He was sleeping soundly next to me with his arm across my stomach.

It was only a little after seven in the morning according to my clock, so I knew that he must have come sometime last night. I remember my body trembling, and I remember closing my eyes and seeing Ethan's face. What I don't remember is changing my clothes and crawling under the covers. Hopefully, my mom helped me with that, and not Brad.

I turned to face him, and for the first time in a long time, I felt something for him, deep down inside. I knew that it was my repressed feelings that were surfacing. I knew that these weren't new feelings.

My brain was on overload still from my trip and every emotion that I could possibly feel my body was allowing me to. No matter how deep down I pushed my feelings for Brad, they always managed to surface eventually, if only for a moment.

My body took on a tingle, and I suddenly had a flashback to the last time he kissed me. It was graduation day, in the restaurant bathroom. I closed my eyes to try and repress that moment from memory, knowing what followed, but my brain was being persistent. My memory was even clearer with my eyes closed.

I remember thinking that it was wrong, what I was doing was wrong. I'm not sure if I realized it at the time, but it wasn't the kiss that made things wrong. It was the move. It was leaving him that was wrong. Brad had done nothing but show me his love for the entire time I had known him. Whether it had been through his supportive friendship or otherwise, all he had ever shown me was love.

I had kicked him to the curb. I had pushed him away. My life wouldn't be the same without him in it. My life would be less than it is without him in it. I wouldn't want that life, and that's the life I have been living these past few months. A life without Brad. A life without Ethan. I life that I didn't even feel that I was living. I had been going through the motions every day, but I had been dead inside.

I was ready to start living again. I was ready to move on with my life, no matter who was or wasn't planning on being in it. Ethan is my better half. He may not be a part of my life anymore, but there was still the other part of me that wanted to live, to move forward, and to rebuild my life. That part of me was going to win this battle. It may take a little glue, but I was going to repair my heart.

I felt his hand graze my cheek, and I opened my eyes. I know that I had been in my own world for a few minutes, and I had needed that. I had needed to get my head on straight. I needed to figure out exactly what it was that I wanted. Opening my eyes and staring into his, I knew. This is what I wanted, what I needed.

"Good morning, sunshine. Glad you're back."

"Back?" It took me a minute to realize that he was talking about my trip. I had been entranced with my previous thought that I had almost forgotten that I had even gone away. "Yeah. I'm back."

That's when he kissed me. He must have known that I wanted him to. His body must have sensed what my body was screaming in that moment.

We had shared a number of stolen kisses over the years. This felt different. This felt right. If it wasn't for my mom bursting through the door to see if we were up and ready for breakfast, it would have been the best kiss we had ever shared.

"Sorry, I didn't realize that I needed to knock. Breakfast is ready when you two are." She spoke fast and disappeared faster. I knew that she was embarrassed and so was I. I had never been caught making out in my bed before. It was a different feeling, and it caused me to laugh uncontrollably.

"What is so funny? I think your mom is gonna want to have a talk with us about the birds and the bees now."

That made me laugh even harder, and I wasn't able to speak. I tried to calm down but I kept picturing my mom's face when she caught sight of us. It was a cross between shock and embarrassment. She acted like we were in the middle of doing something else. That thought alone was enough to make me stop laughing immediately.

"She's going to be fine. It was probably just a shock to her system. She knew you were here, right?"

"Yeah. She let me in last night. I hung around and waited for you to wake up but you never did, so she told me I could just crash here."

"What time did you get here?"

"Natalie called as she was pulling out of your driveway. I rushed over to make sure you were okay, but you were already asleep."

Wow! He came as soon as he knew I was home. He knew that I wouldn't be okay, and he rushed to my side. He waited and waited for me to wake up on my own, and when I didn't, he made sure he was here this morning. I needed time to process this information. We had only started talking again a few weeks ago. He was acting as if we had never even been apart. As if I had never pushed him away, and destroyed our friendship. He was acting as if he had forgiven me.

"Oh!" That was all I could muster at that moment. Yesterday, it had felt like the world was crashing in around me. Today, I wake up to find Brad in my bed. It's like my life did a 180 degree turn in less than twenty four hours. Is that even possible?

"So, should we go join your mom for breakfast? I'm sure she's wondering where we are."

"Yeah. I could definitely eat." Like I had it cued up and ready to sound, my stomach growled. It caused me to chuckle, and that was the first time I had felt at peace and happy in the last three months, maybe longer.

After eating a very tense breakfast with my mom and sister, I knew that it was time for Brad to go. I needed to start picking up the pieces of my life so that I could start putting them all back together. Today was going to be the first day of the next chapter. Today was a new beginning. It was also the end of a lot of things. Today was the day that I was finally going to forgive myself for the damage that I had caused to myself and to everyone around me. Whether I did it on purpose or not, it was time to make my amends. I had to start with myself.

First on my list was to find a job. It didn't have to be anything special, just a way to bring in some money. If I wasn't going to be taking classes again for another couple of months, then I needed to fill my time somehow. If I didn't, I would probably never be able to move on. Too much time spent alone would allow me the opportunity to overanalyze every little aspect of my life. That was something that I did not want to do anymore.

I showered and dressed in a skirt and nice top. I wasn't trying to dress up or to impress anyone. I just wanted to look presentable. I took the time to straighten out my curls and pin my hair back off my face. I even took a couple extra minutes on my makeup. I wanted to look natural but pretty at the same time. Once I was done, I felt pretty.

The last thing I reached for was my jewelry box. I hadn't opened it since moving back in with my mom. I could see the dust that was building up on the top of the lid. I could feel the tension in my neck, and my breathing sped up as I reached for the latch. I knew that the second I opened that box, that I would see the earrings that Ethan had bought me, amongst other items. The only thing that wasn't in that box was the engagement ring that I had given back to him.

I flipped the latch and opened the lid. I was right, the earrings were taunting me the second I saw them. I wanted to wear them but I knew that I wasn't quite ready to take that step yet. Instead, I reached for the diamond earrings that my mom had gotten me for a birthday present a few years back and the emerald ring that Brad had given me.

As I slipped the ring on my finger, it feels cold and unnatural. I had worn that ring for years without removing it but a few times. In those few moments without it, my hand had felt empty, naked. Putting on that ring for the first time in a year, I should have felt something, anything. All I felt was the cold metal that encompassed my finger.

I let the feeling pass and slipped my earrings in. I was dressed to impress and ready to go out and find myself a job. I took one final look at myself in the mirror before snagging up my phone off the charger and heading downstairs. I had a voicemail and a text waiting for me, both from Natalie.

Natalie: Just wanted to make sure we were still on for coffee later today.

We must have made plans while I was zoned out yesterday. I remember talking with her on the ride to my house, but I don't remember what we had talked about. I had been too far inside of my own head to notice anything that was going on around me.

Her voicemail was to remind me of our coffee date. She sounded worried. It's hard to tell someone's tone from a text, but her tone was undeniable in her voicemail. She was hesitant and worried. Well, she would see the new me in a few hours and all her worry would melt away. Hopefully.

I found a job at the first place I stopped. I had never dreamed of being a barista at a coffee shop. The manager was nice and I was pretty sure that he recognized me as a regular customer, so he took a chance on me and hired me on the spot. It didn't pay much and the hours weren't very good, but it was a start, I guess.

I was close to campus, so instead of driving home and sitting around until it was time for me to meet up with Natalie, I decided to take a walk around. The afternoon was warm and the campus was always a beautiful sight when the flowers were starting to bloom again. The colder months made it seem void of life, but I knew that today would be different.

I parked in the student lot knowing that my parking sticker would keep me from being towed and got out. I immediately had a flashback to the first time I had stepped foot on the campus. Ethan and I had been dropping off some paperwork and enrolling me in a few classes. He had given me the grand tour that day of the entire campus, from one end to the other.

I decided in that moment that I was going to take that tour again. I headed straight for the athletic building remembering that was where we had started. I was about two buildings away when the tennis courts came into view, and I could see that practice was going on. I thought about stopping and watching, but I wasn't sure that I was ready to see my coach, so I detoured around the courts and circled back once they were behind me.

Walking up to the athletic building was a whole other challenge in itself. The last time I had been at this end of campus had been over the summer, when I had come to talk with my coach. The day I had broken the news to him about not being released to play was probably the hardest day of my life, at that point anyway.

I took a sharp left turn and started to walk towards the other end of the campus. I was glad that I had settled on flats when I had gotten dressed that morning. If I had gone with the pumps that I knew looked better with the skirt, I would have been regretting that decision right about now. Campus was at least a mile from one end to the other, and I was pretty sure that my legs would have given out before that if I had worn the pumps.

I took a right turn after the next building and found myself back at the tennis courts. I was walking the path that Ethan and I had taken that day long ago, and forgotten that we had walked to the courts. Before I could change my mind about watching, I found myself standing just outside the fence.

My body tensed up when I saw Coach Jones, my assistant coach, wave to me. He started in my direction, and before I knew it, I was inside the fence and headed towards him as well. I knew that no one harbored any bad feelings for me and that I was always welcome here, but I also knew that I had let my team down. I was the one harboring feelings of hatred for the sport.

"Becca. So nice to see you." He wrapped me in a hug the second I was within arm's reach. I immediately felt the pain in my shoulder and cringed, but held back the scream that was trying to break free of my lungs. "So, how have you been?"

"Fine, I guess. How's the team this year?"

"We've got a couple of new faces but it's pretty much the same team as last year. We miss you around here, and I don't just mean on the team. We've missed that positive attitude you used to bring to practice."

Positive attitude? Where did I leave that exactly? Oh! I must have forgotten to take it with me when I was released from the hospital. I know for a fact that I haven't been a very positive person over the last year.

"I've missed you guys too."

"So, what brings you to the courts today? Are you here to watch, or did you want to work your shoulder out a little?"

No!

"I was just taking a walk around the campus and stopped to watch for a minute. I actually have to get going. I'm meeting a friend for coffee in a little bit."

"Oh, well, don't be a stranger. We would love to see you more often. You're always welcome to drop by, you know that."

"Of course. I've just been a little busy."

"Okay, well tell Ethan hello for us, and come see us again soon."

Ethan. Just his name alone makes me want to break down and cry but I don't. I won't allow myself. It's not the place or the time to let that happen. I don't want to cry over him anymore. I am moving on.

I kept those thoughts running through my head the entire walk to the cafeteria. I repeat them over and over again. I need to be strong. This is me moving on. This is me starting over. This is me getting my life back. I am going to forgive myself for the things I've done and become a better version of myself, a better person.

Natalie's waiting for me on the couches when I walk through the door. Her excitement is obvious as she flails her arms above her head to make sure that I see her. There is no way I could have missed her, since she is one of only ten people or so in the entire area.

"Hey. I almost didn't see you sitting over here." My attempt at being funny actually worked this time. Natalie threw her head back and laughed loudly. Her laughter echoed off the walls, and the entire room looked over to where we were sitting.

"Sorry. I'm just excited to see you, I guess. You look nice today. What's the special occasion?"

"I went job hunting."

"Really? Did you find anything?"

"Yeah. I got hired at the coffee shop on Broadway that we used to go to all the time. It's not the 'dream job' I was hoping for but it will do for now."

"That's great, Becca. I'll have to make it a point to come in and see you. When do you start?"

"I have to go in tomorrow to fill out some paperwork, and then I start on Monday. He said my training should only last a few days and then I should be on my own. It sounds like it could be a lot of fun."

"Good. You need a little fun in your life right now." She grimaced as she realized what she said. I saw her relax a little when I smiled in return. She was right. I could use a little fun in my life. "So, I take it you're not mad at me for calling Brad last night?"

"No. Why would I be?"

"Well, I knew that you were hurting and I thought that maybe you needed someone to talk to, but I wasn't sure who. I took a chance and thought that maybe you would talk to him since you weren't really talking to me. I know things between you guys are kind of different these days, so I wasn't sure how you would react."

"Things between us are fine. We talked this morning a little but not about anything important. More than anything, it's gonna have to be me reminding myself that I tried the best I could and that I need to move on."

She's smiling at me but not saying anything. I'm not sure what I said, but apparently, it was the right thing. I smiled back at her but when she starts to squeal with excitement, I get really confused. I watched her as her legs starts to bounce and her body starts to shake like she's about to burst.

"What?"

"You talked this morning? Like, as in, he was still at your house this morning? As in, he stayed the night at your house?"

Now I see clearly. She's excited for me. She must think that I have completely moved on, that Brad and I are now a couple or something.

"As in, he was there when I woke up because I slept from the time you dropped me off until early this morning. As in, I wasn't even aware of his presence. As in, you need to calm down before you splinter into a million pieces over nothing."

"It's not nothing, Becca. When I left you yesterday, you were just the shell of the person you used to be. You were empty inside. It's like you were in there, somewhere, but you didn't want to be found. I saw the look on your face when you walked into the baggage claim area, and I was worried I would never get you back. You looked completely broken. Now, here you sit saying things about how you need to 'move on' and telling me that Brad was with you this morning. This isn't nothing. This is progress. This is you getting your life back to the way it used to be. This is you allowing yourself to heal and to forgive yourself. This is *huge!*"

She was right. This was a bigger deal than I really thought it was. Or at least it was a bigger deal than I wanted to make it out to be. I was healing. I was going to get back to the person that I used to be, before I met Ethan. Before he became a part of my life. Before I fell so deeply in love with him that I wasn't sure where he ended and I began. I need to get back to that Becca, for me.

I found a way to change the subject and we talked about wedding details for the next hour or so, until Natalie had to go to her next class. I contemplated finishing my tour of the campus but was feeling emotionally drained, and instead, headed straight for my car. I knew that if I stayed on campus any longer, that I would end up running into someone that I knew, or Ethan knew, and I didn't have the energy to deal with anyone after talking with Natalie for so long.

Chapter Twelve

June 2012

The days and weeks started to fly by. I was working at the coffee shop as much as I could and decided that I would take summer classes to fill the rest of my time. Natalie and I spent almost every free moment together. I was now officially helping her plan her wedding. I hadn't intended on helping her, knowing that I would feel a stabbing pain every now and again, but it just sort of happened, and the pains started to fade the more we planned.

Brad and I are talking on a regular basis. We are back to being the friends that we used to be. I have been leaning on him heavily for the past few months since coming back from England. I thought that maybe he would try and turn things up a notch, but he's been letting me set the pace, and I have been keeping it slow and steady. I know that things would and could be wonderful if we took our relationship to the next level, I'm just not ready.

I know that deep down I've finally forgiven myself for all the crap that happened back in December. I walked in on Natalie and Morgan talking about Ethan the other day. The mention of his name triggered a pain in my heart, but it was milder than it has been in months. I know that I will always love him, and that I will probably still be in love with him for a while, but that it's over between us. I haven't heard a word from him and it's June.

Ting

As I'm walking out of work, I faintly heard my phone alert me to a text. It's hot out, and all I wanted to do is get in my car and crank up the air conditioning. My phone sounds off again, and I give in and stop to dig for it in my purse. I open up Natalie's text immediately when I find my phone. It falls to the ground as the words I read sink in.

Natalie: You just got a delivery here from England?

I know what she's talking about. I never mentioned it to her, and I know that I should have. I tried to bring it up in conversation a couple of times, but it's such a random thing that I never knew quite how to say it.

I pick up my phone from the sidewalk and pop the battery back in. I make a dash toward my car and start cooling it down as I wait for my phone to restart. What do I do? Do I go and pick it up? Do I leave it there? Do I tell her it's a mistake and to send it back?

Before I realize what I'm doing, I have sent her a message that says I'm on my way over. I hear my phone ting with a reply, but I'm already out in traffic. My hands are already shaky, and I need to concentrate on the road ahead of me.

At the first light I reach that's red, I peek at her reply. It's not from Natalie, it's from Ethan. Ethan? I hear a horn blaring, and I look up to see the light is green, and I'm holding up traffic. I toss my phone back into my purse and focus on the road.

I park on the street in front of Natalie and Morgan's house. I pull my phone out and stare at it for a few minutes debating whether or not I should open my waiting text. I'm not sure what he could possibly have to say to me after all this time. I'm not sure what I want him to say to me. I'm not sure I want to even read what he has to say.

I decide against reading the text, hoping Natalie will do it for me. Maybe she will accidentally push the delete button, and I will never have to know what he had to say. That would drive me crazy, probably. Maybe she could just call him and tell him that I don't want him to contact me anymore. But I want to talk to him. Don't I? Isn't this the most important part of closure? Apologizing.

"Natalie?" I holler for her as I walk through the front door. I know she's expecting me, but she's not answering me. I round the corner into the living room and stop dead in my tracks. I can see the package sitting in front of the sofa. She left it for me to open. "Natalie? Where are you?"

Still no answer. I listen for a minute to see if I can hear the shower, but I don't. I don't hear anything. I walk through the kitchen and pop open the door to the garage. Her car is inside, so she has to be here somewhere. She can't just disappear. I walk back into the living room and out the French doors to the backyard. No Natalie.

Finally, I pull my phone out to call her. I see my waiting text from Ethan. I now see that I have another text from Brad. My heart feels heavy. I'm right back to where I was seven months ago. I can see Ethan's face when I told him I was in love with Brad. I can't do this right now.

I can hear Natalie's phone ringing somewhere in the house, so I follow the sound. I walk back through the kitchen and head towards the garage. It's getting louder and louder, and then it stops. I hang up and call her again.

I'm right outside the laundry room when I hear it start to ring again, and it sounds like it's coming from inside. I slowly open the door and drop to my knees.

Her body looks lifeless. I can see a small amount of blood coming from under her head. I reach for her wrist, and her pulse is weak.

I instinctively call 911, but I can't really tell them what's wrong. I wasn't here when it happened, and I don't know enough to tell them what's wrong with her. I can only tell them that she has a faint pulse and that I'm pretty sure she's breathing. I hang up the phone when I hear the ambulance getting close. I meet them at the front door and direct them to the laundry room.

Before I know what to do they are loading her up and taking her to the hospital. I know that I need to do something, call someone, everyone, but I can't. My feet are cemented to the ground, staring at where I just found Natalie. I'm unable to move, to breathe, to comprehend what just happened. The sound of the sirens from the ambulance as it pulls away from Natalie's house kick-starts my system again.

I grab my phone and dial Morgan's number right away. I get his voicemail, and as soon as I hear the beep I start rambling. I don't want to tell him in a voicemail. I don't want to leave that kind of information on his machine. I want to talk to him, but I have no choice. I leave the message and tell him to meet me at the hospital.

I call Natalie's parents' house next. Her mom answers the phone and, through the tears that have now started to fall, I tell her what's going on. I don't know much, but I tell her what I do know and tell her what hospital.

I'm still standing and staring at the floor when I call Brad. I know that I need to go, that I need to get to the hospital, but I still can't move. I'm staring at the small blood pool on the floor, the laundry basket full of clothes that is tipped over on its side with clothes spilling out, unfolded.

"Becca! Are you there?"

Brad's voice brings me out of my nightmare and back into reality. It's still a nightmare, but I need to start dealing with it. I need to take action and move. That's what I do. I quickly tell Brad what happened and what hospital. I hang up before he can respond. I'm in my car and driving down the road when I remember the reason that I went to Natalie's to begin with.

Ethan.

I don't have time to go back. I don't have time to think about Ethan. I don't have time to think about the photo. I need to get to the hospital. I need to get to Natalie. I need to focus on my driving. The tears are flowing freely, the floodgates opened. I wipe my eyes with the back of my hand, but it only makes it worse. I know that if I'm not careful, that I will end up in a hospital bed next to her, so I pull over.

After rummaging through the glove compartment, I find the tissues that I was looking for. I quickly clean my face up and wipe away the last remnants of my mascara. The hospital is only minutes away. I pull myself together and pull back on the road. I just need to make it there before I start to lose it again. I need to be strong, for Natalie.

The waiting room is full of people, none of which I recognize. I must be the first to arrive, and the thought of that scares me. I approach the nurse's station with caution and tell them my situation. The only thing they can tell me is that Natalie is back being seen by the doctors. They can't tell me what's wrong with her, if she's conscious, if she's even alive. I'm not family.

Brad is the first through the ER doors. He spots me and heads in my direction. There are no seats left, so he crouches in front of me and takes my hands. I'm not crying, but I feel like I might any second. His presence soothes me in a way that most things can't. I know that he's only touching my hands, but I can feel his touch everywhere, especially in my heart.

Before I can even speak, Morgan rushes through the doors and up to the desk. I can see that he's panicked. I would never want to get the voicemail that he got. After talking, or rather yelling, at the nurse I had already spoken to, he spots us and heads toward us.

"They won't tell me anything. What the hell happened, Becca?"

"I don't really know. She sent me a text and I told her I would come over, and when I got there, I couldn't find her anywhere. I called her cell and heard it ringing, so I followed the sound. I found her on the floor, unconscious. It looked like she may have hit her head, there was a little blood. I checked for a pulse and called 911."

I held back all emotion while I told him what happened. It was the only way I would have been able to get it out. If I allowed myself to cry, I wouldn't be able to stop again. It must have sounded like I was reading my grocery list.

We waited for another fifteen minutes before Natalie's parents finally arrived. I waved to them, but neither of them saw me. They talked to the nurse and were shown through a set of doors. The only thing I could do was stare. I knew they would be shown back. I knew they would be given information. I knew that we would be left in the dark to wonder and worry. I knew all of this, yet I still wanted to run after them before the door clicked closed behind them.

We waited for what felt like hours to hear something, anything, from Natalie's parents or the doctors. There was radio silence. No one was saying anything. No one would tell us anything. Then, Morgan got a text. It didn't say much, but it gave us hope.

Natalie is awake and talking. Go home and get some rest. She has to stay overnight. Will call later.

We went our separate ways, reluctantly leaving through the front doors together. I knew that we would all be back first thing in the morning to check up on her. I knew that none of us were going to sleep well. I knew that something was wrong with her, and that there was more information that they were not sharing with us right now. I knew all of this, yet I went home because I was told to. I knew all of this, and I knew that there was nothing I could do about any of it except wait to hear what her parents and the doctors had to say. I felt completely helpless.

It was dark when I finally pulled up in front of my house. The lights were on, and I could see my mom in the kitchen, moving around quickly. She was probably making dinner, unaware of everything else that was happening right now.

A set of headlight pulled up behind me, temporarily blinding me. I shut my car off and got out to find Brad getting out of his car. I didn't say anything, and I didn't need to. He pulled me into his chest and wrapped his arms tightly around me. I sank deep into his body and let him hold me for a few minutes.

I was on the verge of crying again. My body was tired, my mind was tired, and I needed to lay down. I hadn't mentioned the package to Brad or Morgan. It was not important at the time, and now I had no idea how to bring it up in conversation with Brad. We don't fight, we don't argue. This wouldn't cause us to start, but it would cause tension. I didn't need that right now.

I knew that Morgan would find it when he got back to their house, but I didn't really care. It would be the last thing on his mind. He might say something in the morning at the hospital, and I was hoping that if he did, Brad wouldn't be around. I felt like I was keeping something from him, but I also felt like it was the right thing to do. The only thing that has ever come between us before is my relationship with Ethan. I didn't want to reopen that wound.

We made our way inside and talk to my mom for a while. It was close to midnight by the time we filled her in on everything, and she excused herself for bed. With her being a nurse, I thought that she would offer some kind of explanation to the situation. Give us a few "maybe this is what's going on" scenarios. She said nothing. I figured that meant it was worse than we feared.

Brad and I crawled into bed shortly after my mom. It wasn't unusual for him to stay the night at this point. He was here most days and a few nights a week. He keeps a toothbrush here and deodorant. We still haven't taken our relationship to the next level but at this point, I'm not sure I'm ready to. After the reaction I had to my photograph arriving today, I know that I'm still not really over my feelings for Ethan. Maybe I never really will be?

Thinking about Ethan while I'm wrapped up in Brad's arms feels like I'm cheating on him. He has no idea what I'm thinking about, but I do. I know that I have a clear image of Ethan's painful expression while looking at my portrait. I know that I'm thinking about that same portrait sitting in Natalie and Morgan's living room, waiting for me to pick it up.

That's when it hits me that I never read his text from earlier today. I'm not sure if I want to read it, but my curiosity is peaked. Why now? Why is he sending me a message now? What about the last six months?

I slip out of Brad's arms without waking him and rummage through my purse in the dark. I slowly open my door and step into the hall. My hands are shaking. I can feel my heart beating rapidly in my chest. My pulse is racing, and I wonder if it's out of fear or anticipation.

I try to turn my phone on and realize that the battery is dead. I head downstairs to plug it in and wait. I give it only five minutes or so before I power it up. Once I am able to open my messages, I do and immediately start to cry.

Morgan: Natalie has a brain tumor. You need to come back to the hospital ASAP. They are doing surgery at noon tomorrow.

Ethan's message is long forgotten after reading the one from Morgan. After I'm able to compose myself, I leave my phone on the counter to charge and go wake up Brad. I need to get to the hospital, and there is no way I will be able to drive by myself.

We arrive at the hospital and even though visiting hours are over, they let us in to see Natalie. Her parents are by her bed, along with Morgan. She's sitting up, smiling, as if nothing is wrong. Her smile brings tears to my eyes, and I wonder if I'm ever going to be able to stop crying.

She's extremely pale. She has a large bandage wrapped around her head. She has machines hooked up to her everywhere. She's wearing one of those oxygen tubes that they stick up your nose and around your ears. She looks sick, yet she's smiling.

I can hear the beeping of a monitor. I can hear the whoosh of the breathing machine. I can hear the hum of the other machines. What I don't hear is Natalie calling my name while I take in my surroundings.

"Becca!"

"Sorry." I move closer to her and take a seat in an open chair by her bed. "So, what are the doctors saying?"

"Well, it's not good news. I have a tumor growing in my cerebellum. Supposedly, that can cause me to lose control of some muscle functions. I remember my legs giving out and then hitting my head, so I must have fallen."

She said it so plainly. She said it like it was no big deal. It was *definitely* a big deal. They are going to cut her head open in the morning. She is having surgery on part of her brain! "Okay. So, after they remove the tumor, what happens?"

"She'll need to stay here for a while." Natalie's dad was trying to sound strong, but I could hear the sadness in his voice. "They will need to monitor her breathing to make sure that they didn't damage anything when they removed the tumor. There's a chance that they may not be able to get all of it in one surgery, so they may have to go back in a second time in a few days."

I can see Natalie's mom crying out of the corner of my eye. She's standing tall and letting her tears fall. She's trying to be strong for Natalie, for her family. I, on the other hand, am crying freely and sniffling like a baby.

"I will be fine, Becca. The doctors say that I was lucky to have found it as soon as I did. Normally, a tumor like this can go undetected for a while."

"How long do they think you've had it? Didn't you have any symptoms?"

"Yeah, but I didn't know they were symptoms of a brain tumor. I was nauseated a lot and have gotten a few headaches lately, but I thought that maybe I was just fighting a virus. For a minute we thought we were pregnant since I was always feeling like I was going to throw up in the morning."

Brad quickly changed the subject. I never thought that I would be so excited to talk about having babies and getting married. We stayed only for a few more minutes before I gave Natalie a long, tight squeeze, and wished her luck. She knew that I would be in the waiting room with Morgan and her parent's tomorrow afternoon. She knew that I would be waiting for her, praying for her.

Chapter Thirteen

Natalie's surgery took almost six hours. When we finally heard that she made it though and that they were almost positive that they got everything was when I breathed a sigh of relief. I could see the relief on Natalie's parents face. I could see the relief on Morgan's face. I could feel the tension in the room melt away. Natalie was going to be okay.

I left the hospital before she woke up. I was exhausted and needed some rest, so when they said that she probably wouldn't wake up until the next morning, I headed home to bed. Brad was waiting for me when I got there. He had spoken to my professors for me and picked up my homework. There was no way that I was going to be able to go to class today or even tomorrow.

I passed out on my bed before I even took my shoes off. The weight on my shoulders felt like it had been lifted. I was light as a feather and floated freely into the land of dreams. I felt Brad remove my shoes and cover me up. I was even aware that he didn't crawl in next to me, but I didn't have the energy to open my eyes or speak.

"I love you so much, Becca." I heard his words and felt him kiss my forehead before I passed back out.

Tight arms wrapped around me from behind. I could feel his nipple ring pressing into my shoulder. His heart was beating rapidly against my back. I knew who was standing behind me, and I was scared to turn around.

I knew his smile would make my insides melt like butter, and I wasn't sure if I was ready for that. I knew that one look at him and I would never want to leave his arms again. I didn't need to open my eyes to know who was holding me, but I did anyway.

Instinctively, I started to twist my ring. I could see Ethan standing inside his gallery, staring at my photograph, the one he took of me. His eyes are vacant but the emotion on his face is very real. The pain is real.

I feel cold, and I have to look down to realize that I'm no longer wrapped in his arms. When I look back up, Ethan is staring at me through the window. It's almost as if he's staring into my soul, but he's not really seeing me. His lips move, and I know that he's saying something, but I can't hear him. Then the woman with the red hair appears from behind him and puts her hand on his shoulder like she's trying to console him.

Who is this woman? I've seen her before—when I was in England. I am in England. I've been here before. I've lived this nightmare before. Why does this feel so real?

I awake with a start. Brad's next to me with his arm lying across my waist. I slip out of bed without disturbing him and head for the bathroom. The sun's not up yet, so I know it's still early. I jump in the shower and start to get myself ready for the day. The dream is still fresh in my mind and so is the fact that I have avoided Ethan's text.

I start a pot of coffee, and once I have a steaming cup, I head to the back porch to enjoy the sunrise. It's the most beautiful sight to watch the sun coming up over the Santa Catalina Mountain. The only thing prettier is watching it set over them with someone you love.

My phone is sitting on the table in front of me. I know that I need to read his message. I know that I will drive myself crazy until I know what he wants. It's been six months since I've had any contact with him. As far as I know, he doesn't even know that I went to England. My mom and Natalie promised not to tell him, and the only other people who knew were Morgan and Brad. I can't imagine either of them told him.

I close my eyes and snag my phone off the table. I take a few deep breaths before opening his text. No matter what it says, I know that I will have a hard time reading it. I know that as I read it, I will hear his voice speaking to me. I know that this changes things, my feelings for him. I can feel my heart beginning to swell with love for him just for sending me a text.

Ethan: It's been delivered to Natalie's house for you.

So he knew that I ordered the photograph. Did he know that I was in England? Did he know that I was at his show? Did he see me in the gallery? I need answers. I need to know what to do next. Do I text him back? It's been two days since he sent me that message. Does he think I'm ignoring him?

I have to talk to Natalie. She'll know what to do. *Crap!* Natalie. I wonder how she's doing this morning. She won't be up to talking about Ethan. She may not even be awake yet. I need to get to the hospital and check on her.

The sun is starting to peek over the mountains now, filling the sky with light and announcing the start of the day. What will today hold for me?

I hear my phone alert me to a new text as I pull into the hospital parking lot. Brad is probably wondering where I am. Maybe it's my mom. Whoever it is has to wait because I have to turn my phone off before I reach Natalie's floor. Intensive care doesn't allow you to have your cell phones on.

Walking into the lobby, I immediately spot Morgan and Natalie's parents. Everyone is on their phones, so I keep going towards the elevator bank. I'm sure I will see them when they head back up to Natalie's room. The elevator arrives on the fifth floor, and I approach the nurse's station and wait for someone to open the doors for me.

"Can I help you?"

"May I please go back and see Natalie Johanson? I should be on the approved list of visitors. My name is Rebecca Blake."

Her face tells me that something is wrong. Immediately, I flash back to walking through the lobby. Natalie's parents look like they have been crying. Morgan looks angry. Something had happened. How did I miss that?

"I'm sorry, but she cannot have any visitors right now. Her parents just went downstairs. You should probably go and find them."

I head back to the elevators in a trance. Something is wrong, really wrong. Why could she not have any visitors? I need to find Morgan. I power my phone back up so that I can call and find out where he is.

The elevator arrives in the lobby as my phone alerts me to a waiting text message. I open up my box to find three new messages, the first of which is from Morgan. I also have one from Brad and one from my mom. I open Morgan's message and collapse onto the floor of the elevator as the doors open. I see Brad's face for a split second before everything goes black around me.

Morgan: Natalie's not doing well get here ASAP

The lobby is full of friends and family when I finally come to. I'm laying down on one of the couches with my head in my mom's lap. I can see Brad and Morgan talking in the corner. Lainey and Jill are coming through the front entrance as I sit up and they rush over to me.

"What's going on, Becca. Morgan sent us both a text to get here quickly but didn't tell us why. What's wrong with Natalie?"

Lainey was talking so fast that it took me a moment to comprehend what she was saying. No one really knew what was going on with Natalie. Everything had happened so fast that I hadn't called anyone, and I'm sure it was the last thing on Morgan's mind.

I started from the beginning and gave them the shortened version. I told them about finding her in the laundry room, and I told them about the tumor and the surgery. I didn't know much after that. There were about twenty of us or so, and we all stopped talking when Natalie's parents walked back in the room. Natalie's dad was holding up Natalie's mom who was crying and having a hard time walking.

It took him a moment to compose himself while we all stared at him and waited. He cleared his throat twice before he was finally able to look up and make eye contact with anyone.

"Natalie took a turn for the worse last night. We've just finished speaking with the doctors, and it looks like there are going to be some complications from the surgery. They put her in a medically induced coma so that her body can rest, but they are going to have to do surgery again."

Everyone was quiet. Stunned silence was the best way to describe it. I was afraid to move. I was afraid to speak. The quietest sound would have been able to be heard down the hall and around the corner.

I had questions. How long before the next surgery? How long was the coma going to last? What exactly went wrong? I wanted answers. I needed answers.

I finally excused myself and walked over to where Brad and Morgan were standing. Brad took me in his arms without hesitation. I immediately felt tense, flashing back to my dream once again. When he wrapped his arms around me from behind, I had to pull away. It was too much like my dream. I knew that this was real, and that the dream was just a dream, but the dream had felt real, too real.

"I need fresh air. Morgan, will you come outside with me?"

He didn't answer but instead turned and headed towards the exit. I shot Brad a quick smile and follow Morgan out the front doors of the hospital. He sat down on a bench not far from the entrance, and started to cry. My emotions broke free the second I saw the tears streaming down his face.

We sat there, holding hands and crying together. It was heartbreaking to know that Natalie was sicker than we thought. It was heartbreaking to know that we couldn't see her or talk to her. It was heartbreaking for someone as vibrant and lively as Natalie to be brought down by something as awful as a tumor.

"She's really bad, Becca," Morgan finally spoke as the tears started to subside.

"How bad?" How bad was really bad? I thought a brain tumor was really bad. Could it really be any worse? They said that they got everything. They said she was recovering. Natalie has always had a fighting spirit. She had to make it through this.

"The doctors say that her body is not functioning properly on its own. She had to be put back on her breathing machine, and they are monitoring her heart rate. Apparently, it's erratic. At first, they thought it was from the surgery, that her body was stressed or something. Now, they're really not sure what's going on. They put her in a coma to help her body relax."

I wasn't sure what to say. I knew that no matter what I said or did, nothing was going to change the situation. Nothing was going to help Natalie heal any faster. Nothing was going to help any of us heal any faster. We had to wait and see what the doctors said, to see how Natalie's body reacts. We have to wait until she wakes up.

The hours passed, and slowly, family and friends left the hospital in search of food and prayer. I knew that if I left, something would happen, Natalie's status would change. I was afraid to breathe, afraid to speak, afraid to move an inch, thinking that if I did, she might not make it.

The doctors came down and talked with Natalie's parents a little after dinnertime. Judging by the body language of the doctors, I knew that nothing had changed. They were void of emotion when speaking. Both of them were standing up straight and looking Natalie's dad in the eyes. They exuded confidence from head to toe, but they didn't have me fooled. If they were as confident as they looked, Natalie would be getting better, not staying the same.

As much as I didn't want to, I left the hospital as it got dark. Even Natalie's parents were going home for the night. There was nothing we could do for her, and we all knew it.

I promised to meet Morgan and Brad back up at the hospital in the morning. Brad wanted to come over, but I told him I was going to go straight to bed and that it was pointless. I wanted to go straight to bed. I wanted to sleep, I needed to sleep. What I didn't want or need was to dream.

I knew the dreams would come, and I knew that I would remember them vividly when I woke up the next morning. I wasn't sure that I would be able to handle that. I wasn't sure that my emotions would be able to handle that. I wasn't sure I knew how to handle that. All I could think about as I crawled in bed that night was how I didn't want to dream. How I didn't want to think about Ethan. How I knew that I wouldn't be able to handle it if he controlled my world in my dreams the way he sometimes controls my world when I'm awake.

That was the last thing I remember thinking as I passed out cold.

Chapter Fourteen

Present Day

It was four very long days before Natalie woke up from her coma. As soon as she was able to see visitors, her room filled up quickly. There were family members coming and going. Friends were popping in to see her. She got at least five deliveries of flowers that first day that the nurses brought in for her. Her room was like a revolving door that never stopped moving.

The only constants in the room were her parents, Morgan and me. I barely left the hospital for what ended up being almost a week from beginning to end. I slept in my own bed at night and eventually started leaving to get food, but otherwise I was stationed as close to Natalie as I could be.

The day after she woke up is when things started to go wrong. I was the first to arrive that morning. The doctors and nurses were outside her room and there was a lot of commotion coming from behind her closed door. I knew better than to try and go inside since I wasn't family, so I headed back downstairs toward the cafeteria instead to get some stale coffee.

I sent Morgan a text, letting him know that something was up and to meet me in the cafeteria when he got to the hospital. It took almost ten minutes for him to reply. He was already here, upstairs in Natalie's room. I figured that meant that things had settled down, and that everything was okay to head back up. Boy, was I wrong on both accounts.

Another text immediately followed.

Morgan: Stay there. I will be down soon

That was a bad sign if I ever saw one.

I waited for what felt like forever. When I finally spotted Morgan walking down the hall, I realized that something was wrong immediately. If he was trying to mask how he was feeling, he was doing a horrible job. The pain was evident in the way he walked, his posture. Mainly, it was evident by the solemn look on his face.

The doctors had warned us that Natalie may never be the same as she was. Once she woke up, they would know more about her "condition," they kept saying. Either I was in the dark or her "condition" was supposed to be apparent to those around her. I knew that there was a reason she was in the hospital. I knew that they had removed a very large tumor from her brain. I knew a lot about what was going on, or so I thought.

Morgan took a seat next to me, crashing into the chair with a loud thud. I knew it was bad even before he opened his mouth. I knew that her situation, her "condition" had worsened. I knew that whatever was going on, whatever he was about to tell me, was not good news.

"The doctors don't think that they got everything. Her behavior is erratic, and her moods have been fluctuating like crazy since you left last night. I knew something was wrong when she woke up this morning and didn't know who I was."

Crap! Crap! Crap!

It was worse than I thought. I didn't know what to say. I wanted to tell him that everything was going to be fine, but I knew deep down that it wasn't. I knew that we were losing her, that we have possibly lost her already. So instead of talking, we sat in silence and let it all sink in. The pain, the sadness, the reality of the situation. We let it sink in so deep that the tears started to come before either of us knew that we were crying. That's how we spent the morning.

The days began to blur together. Days turned into weeks, and the weeks turned into a month. Before I knew it, it was July, and there was still no change in Natalie's status. She was awake. She was coherent. She was still not herself.

Between work and school and visiting Natalie every day, I was completely exhausted. Morgan was as close to having a mental breakdown as I was. I think he was taking all of this the hardest. The woman he loved was no longer here. The vibrant, happy, fun-loving woman he fell in love with, was nowhere to be seen. In her place was a bitter, angry introvert.

We were all still asking why? Why did this happen? The doctors didn't have any answers for us. They couldn't explain her change in mood. They couldn't explain much actually. They checked and rechecked her scans to make sure they got the entire tumor. Everything was coming back clear. The only reason they have been keeping her for observation is because she is showing signs of heart failure on the monitors.

They've done tests and blood work and everything has come back normal. If you watch the machines she's hooked up to, you would think she was normal. Her body is acting completely normal, except the random beeping of the heart monitor every few minutes.

I'm not an expert, far from it, but it sounds like her heart stops for a few seconds and then starts again. The really weird part is that when it starts again, it's working really hard and pumping really fast. The doctors can't seem to figure it out. They say all they can do is monitor her and see what happens.

I don't like playing the wait and see game. I actually hate it. I just left the hospital. I stopped in to check on Natalie after work and was greeted with a plastic cup to the face. Natalie was throwing a tantrum, again. This was a huge part of the "New Natalie" that I was not a fan of. Either she was in a rage, or she had no clue who I was. It was a toss-up as to what I would walk in to on any given day.

I need to shake it off and go to bed. I have a test in the morning, and I work again tomorrow. I was planning on visiting Natalie in-between the two, but I wasn't sure if I was welcome or not. I'll go anyway. Her tantrums normally only last a few hours. She won't even remember tomorrow.

Fireworks are starting to go off as I pull in the driveway. I forgot what day it was for a minute. I can see a red starburst blast throughout the night sky over the neighboring house. It reminds me of last year's festivities. I spent the day with Natalie and Morgan and Ethan. Now, here I am, alone. Well, not totally alone. Brad is waiting inside for me.

Without even speaking, he grabs my hand the second I'm through the door and pulls me into the backyard. The show is amazing. I cannot even begin to describe how beautiful the fireworks look with the mountains as a backdrop. Every time one goes off, the landscape behind it is illuminated. It's the most wonderful sight.

I rest my head back against Brad's chest as he wraps his arms around me. This is my solitude. He is my rock; he always has been, and I have no idea how I would make it through this without him. I don't know how I would have made it through most of my life's "downs" without his support, without him by my side, holding my hand, telling me everything is going to be okay.

The show lasted about twenty minutes. The finale was amazing. So many fireworks, so many colors. For a moment I got lost in the sight, forgot about my day and let my mind rest. It was perfect, until it ended.

Inside, waiting for me, was dinner. Brad had a way of softly attacking me. If he thought that I needed to eat, he would surprise me by cooking. If he thought that I needed to relax, he would surprise me with a bath. Most of the time, his surprises were spot on, like he knew what I needed before I knew. Sometimes, it felt like an attack. Today, he was spot on, and as I caught the faintest aroma coming from the kitchen, my stomach made a very loud, very approving noise.

We talked casually over dinner. We never talked about anything important anymore. We tried to keep things light by talking about the things that mattered the least in life. Today's topic was gas prices. Like I said, in comparison to what was really going on, gas prices didn't matter one bit to either of us.

Brad had stopped going to the hospital a few weeks ago. He never said anything about it, he just stopped. It had been bugging me for a while as to why he stopped, but I never found the right time to bring it up. That's not true. There had been plenty of available opportunities to ask. I just wasn't sure I wanted to hear the answer.

"So, not to change the subject of our *very* important conversation, but I need to ask you something." I was hesitant and I knew that he could tell. There was no real easy way to ask this. The entire situation was incredibly sensitive.

"Okay. I think I know what you're going to ask me and before you do, I want to say something."

Crap! This conversation is not going to be a good one. Maybe I can still back out of it? Nope! I can see the determination in his eyes.

"I need you to know that I love you, more than I will ever be able to put into words. I need you to know that no matter what happens to Natalie, no matter the outcome, that I will still be there for you. Do you understand?"

"Yeah, of course. But, Brad…"

"No. I need you to just listen for a minute. Natalie and I agreed to never talk about this with you, but I think that you need to know. I think that Natalie would want to be the one to tell you, but I'm not even sure she remembers any of it. So, I need you to listen, without interrupting me, without asking questions, without jumping to conclusions. I need you to understand that everything that was said and done, was done out of love, from the bottom of our hearts. Can you do that for me? Can you just listen for a few minutes?"

I shake my head because my heart is in my throat preventing me from saying anything. This is going to be really bad. I'm not going to like what he has to say, and he knows it. The fact that he's avoiding eye contact with me should have been my first clue, but what I was focused on right now had nothing to do with Brad. The only thing I can feel is the pounding of my heart, and the fear that he's about to break it.

"Becca, I…"

My cell starts ringing, and at the same time, his does. I jump, startled out of my current state and reach for my phone. I look down to see Morgan's face and before I can bring myself to answer it, Brad grabs my phone.

"He can wait. I really need to get this off my chest."

"Fine, but who was calling you?"

"Morgan. He must have put us on three way."

"Brad. Why would he put us on a three-way call when we are always together? Something has to be going on, something important. I'm gonna call him back and then we can finish our conversation."

I think he knew what I was thinking. It was all I ever thought about. The phone call that I never wanted to get, the one I feared would come. I didn't want this call to be that call. I wasn't ready for that call, but I knew this was it, and I think Brad did too.

"I would rather tell you this before you call him back."

"I know, and I would much rather have this conversation than the one I'm about to have. Brad, no matter what you say, no matter what happened, you have to know that I love you, and that our relationship is stronger that whatever it is you have to tell me. We will survive this, whatever it is. My fear right now is that I need to get back to the hospital, and the longer we talk about this, the less time I have to get there. Are you coming with me?"

I could see his brain working overtime, contemplating whether or not he should come with me. "Yeah. I'll drive so you can call him back."

We were in the car and on the road in minutes. I pulled up Morgan's number and hit send. It took me three tries to actually hit the button I was shaking so badly. Either we were going to get good news or…well, I can't think about the other option.

It went straight to voicemail. I didn't leave a message, and when I checked, he hadn't left one for me. The signs were not good. Pulling into the hospital parking lot, I felt like I was going to be sick. Walking through the front entrance, I knew I was going to be sick.

I darted down the hall and around the corner. With no bathroom in sight, I went for the closest trash can and threw up the little bit of dinner I had managed to eat. I didn't feel better, but I had nothing left in me, so I was safe for a few minutes. I made my way back to the entrance to find Brad, and as I rounded the corner, I saw that Morgan had already found him.

I couldn't tell what was going on. Morgan had his back to me and Brad's face was shielded by Morgan's body. They were talking in hushed tones, and immediately halted their conversation when Brad saw me approaching.

Morgan slowly turned around and that's when I saw his face. I knew immediately that we had lost her. His eyes were puffy and bloodshot from crying, and the remnants of his tears were still streaking down his face. I reached for the nearest wall and slowly slid to the floor. My friend, my confidant…gone.

I brought my knees to my chest and rested my head on them. I was aware that I was crying. I was aware that Brad had settled next to me on the floor. I was even aware that there were people passing by, probably staring. What I wasn't aware of was how empty I would feel. That's how I felt, mind, body and soul. Empty.

I sat down in the front row, mom on one side of me and Brad on the other. They each held my hand as the pastor began to speak. I tried to tune in, to listen to what he was saying, but it was all a blur. The only thing I could think about was whether or not Ethan was in the church.

Brad squeezed my hand and brought me back to reality, a reality that I didn't want to live in right now. It was my turn to speak. I had promised Morgan and Natalie's parents that I would give part of the eulogy. Why? Why had I done that to myself? I knew that there was no way to put into words the way we were all feeling.

I opened my purse and pulled out my speech. I was about to close it when I caught sight of the envelope Morgan had given me at the hospital. It was from Natalie. I would recognize her handwriting anywhere. She had written me a letter. A letter I had yet to read. A letter I was scared to read. Which Natalie had written the letter?

I stood and made my way to the podium. I locked my eyes on the pastors to avoid looking at Natalie. I knew that I would lose it if I looked at her again. I was holding on by a thread as it was, and if this speech didn't break me, looking at her would.

I cleared my throat and looked out at the massive crowd. I was looking for him, and I knew it. When I spotted him, I allowed our eyes to connect. I may not be his biggest fan right now, but he was going to help me get through this.

"Natalie was one of the most vibrant people I have ever had the pleasure of knowing. She took hold of whatever she wanted and threw herself into head on. I never understood how she was able to do that. I never understood how fear was never a problem for her. It was almost as if she had no fear when it came to life. She only knew how to live."

I had to pause. I could feel my emotions creeping up on me. I could feel the tears running down my cheeks, and the only thing I could do to control them was stare at Ethan.

"Natalie and I met when we were seventeen. Since then, we've shared a lot of ups and down. We've gotten each other through a lot of hard times. Most of all, we made a lot of great memories. That's how I'm choosing to remember my friend today. I'm choosing to remember the good times we've shared, the small things that made her one of my best friends. I'm choosing to remember the late nights studying together, the afternoon coffee meetings on campus. I'm choosing to hold on to these memories and take them with me when I leave this church. Why you ask? There is one thing in life that is certain, and its death. Today, instead of mourning the death of my friend, I am choosing to celebrate her life, who she was, and how she lived. Natalie wouldn't want us to shed tears of sorrow but tears of joy. She would want us to remember the good times and laugh. She would want us to go on living and that's what we have to do.

"Let's keep Natalie's vibrant spirit alive by celebrating who she was today. She would have wanted us to throw her a party, not a funeral, and if she was here to see us crying for her, she would scold each and every one of us." That got a laugh from the audience. I knew it was true, and I knew that as brave as I was being that Natalie was probably looking down on me, scolding me for crying. "So, is there anyone else who would care to share a story about Natalie? Anyone who would like to say a few nice words about the vibrant woman that you had the pleasure of calling your friend?"

It amazed me how many lives Natalie had touched in her short twenty-one years. Over the next thirty minutes or so, person after person went up and took a few minutes to remember Natalie by sharing their fondest memories or stories. Even Brad went up and said a few words which surprised me since I never really thought about him being close with Natalie. I guess his friendship with me had allowed a friendship to blossom between them.

Morgan was the last to go, and I could see that it was hard on him, sharing the memories of the woman who was supposed to be his wife, bear his children, and grow old with him. I couldn't imagine losing Brad, or Ethan for that matter. I couldn't imagine losing anyone else right now. I was in enough pain, but the memories helped. Everyone sharing helped. Until Ethan approached the podium, I held onto that inner peace that had started to take over. In those few moments, it all came to a halt.

"Did you know he was here? I never saw him come in."

I didn't have any words. My voice had disappeared, and it was all I could do to remind myself to breathe. I nodded only once and turned back to Ethan who was staring right at me. I felt Brad reach for my hand, but when he realized that I couldn't hold onto him right now, he released it and let it fall limply back into my lap.

"Natalie and I have known each other for a long time. We even date once. As brief as that encounter was, it was meaningful, and she left a mark on my heart. She was a wonderful person, inside and out. She knew exactly what she wanted out of life, and she went for it. I admired that about her. Her tenacity to work hard until she got what she wanted, what she deserved." He took a moment to let what he said sink in. Before he started to speak again, he turned and directed his attention to Morgan.

"Morgan, you are one lucky man. You had the opportunity to fall in love with a wonderful woman, the opportunity to feel what it's like to be loved completely, wholly and unconditionally. People spend a lifetime looking for that one person that completes them, and you found her in high school. You had the opportunity to love and cherish her for five years. You had the opportunity to feel what it was like to be consumed by someone so much that you weren't quite sure where you ended and she began. It's a love unlike any other and you had that. I cannot tell you how sorry I am that it had to end so soon or so abruptly."

I can see that Morgan is crying, sobbing. I know that Ethan's words are not meant to hurt him, but they are a reminder of what he's lost, who he's lost, and they are not bringing him the comfort that he needs right now. It's time for Ethan to wrap things up. I think his speech may actually be making Morgan feel worse.

"Now, I know all of this is hard for everyone to hear, but there is one more thing I need to share with all of you." *Crap!* He's not going to wrap it up. "Natalie sent me a letter a few weeks ago. She asked me to read this to all of you knowing that I could not deny her this one thing. So, here goes."

It feels like it takes forever for him to pull out the folded up paper from his jacket pocket. It feels like it takes hours for him to unfold it and press it flat enough for him to read. You can tell that it's been read a number of times. From where I'm sitting, I can clearly see a few rips in the paper, and the many different creases that it has. My anxiety is creeping up. What was so important that Natalie had to have Ethan come here and read to all of us?

Crap! Natalie is the reason that Ethan is here. Natalie must have contacted him or told someone to contact him. Natalie was responsible for his presence, and she wasn't here for me to rely on or to yell at. *Damn her!*

Dearest friends and family.

Unglued

I am having Ethan read this to you because I can no longer be with any of you. There are a few things that I need to get off my chest and I need for you all to listen very clearly to what I have to say. You kind of have to, right? You are at my funeral after all. If you're here it's because you cared about me and I cared about you. I was a very lucky woman in life. I was lucky enough to have friends and family like all of you. So I need for you all to do something for me. I need for all of you to stop crying, to help each other grieve quickly and then move on. There is no reason that life cannot move on without me because it will and it will happen quickly. Please don't spend your time crying for me and let life pass you by.

If you knew me at all you would know that I would be upset by that. I made it my life's mission to enjoy each and every day and that's what I need you to do for me, with each other. I have written many of you letters and I know that none of you have read them, except maybe one. Trust me when I say that you need to read those letters. They will help you. They are not good-bye letters. They were written with the intent of helping you move on after I was gone. If you didn't receive a letter it wasn't because I didn't care, it was because I didn't have enough time. Time is something we take for granted each and every day. If you learn anything from me and my short time on this Earth please learn this: there is no time like the present to start building your future.

The future is just around the corner, and you need to be ready for it. I was. I was building my future with the most amazing man and the most amazing friends anyone could ask for—all of you. I love you all dearly. Remember the good times we had and carry me in your hearts always.

Love—Natalie

The church is silent. The only sounds that I could hear were the whimpers and sniffles. Natalie had always been great at silencing a room with her presence, and now she's done it with her absence. I turn to look at Morgan. I'm pretty sure he's about to break down. I can see his body is shaking. I can see the tears that are streaming down his face. I can see the loss, the emptiness. I can feel it too.

Ethan folded his piece of paper back up and gracefully returned to his seat in the back of the room. He was so composed. It was almost as if nothing affected him. How could this not affect him? He just read

Natalie's last words to over a hundred people who are grieving for her, no matter how much she doesn't want us to.

That's when it hit me. The paper was torn. It had been folded and unfolded a bunch of times. It looked like he had read and reread that letter a number of times. He had found a way to numb himself, and Natalie knew that he would be able to do that.

The pastor gave directions to the cemetery and to Morgan and Natalie's house for the luncheon after. This is where I parted ways with my best friend. I promised Morgan that I would handle the luncheon. I needed to get to their house and take care of the caterers. This was where I would say my good-byes to my best friend.

The people filed out of the church, and the only ones left were the paul bearers and me. I asked for a moment alone to say my good-byes. I knew that this would be the last time that I would lay eyes on my friend. I made it quick, not really able to speak. I smoothed back her hair, laid my rose inside the casket with her, and shut the lid just as the pastor returned.

Good-bye, dear friend.

Chapter Fifteen

Walking into Morgan and Natalie's alone immediately brought the flashback that I was fearing. It only lasted a second, but immediately, my eyes were drawn to the laundry room. This is where is all started. The day I found Natalie on the floor, in a small pool of her own blood. That was the beginning of the end.

I forced myself into the kitchen. The caterers would be here in ten minutes, and I needed to at least start setting up some of the things that they brought last night. I pulled platters from the cupboards and the punch bowl from the pantry. I piled everything up high and moved into the dining room to set everything up on the table.

I had asked Morgan to place the extension piece in the middle of the table, but he must have forgotten. I could see it leaning up against the wall in the living room. I set everything down carefully and went to retrieve it. Walking into the living room, something caught my attention out of the corner of my eye. The portrait.

I had almost forgotten about it. When Natalie first got admitted to the hospital, I was too scared to come back and get the portrait. After a while, I forgot about it. Now, here, standing in the living room, facing the still-wrapped package, there was no getting away from it. I needed to clear it out of the living room, of the house, before people came, before Ethan saw it.

Unglued

I made quick work of placing the package in the front closet. I would take it with me when I left for the day, hours from now. There was no way I would be able to forget it. I could feel its presence as I set up the dining room table. I could feel its presence even after the caterers arrived and started setting out the food. I could feel its presence from the upstairs bathroom when I went to fix my makeup before the guests started to arrive. It was almost as if it was pulling me to it, begging me to open it.

I reached in my purse to pull out some lipstick and saw the envelope from Natalie again. She had said that we needed to read them. She said that it would help us to move on. I knew that she was probably right. After all, she was the one I confided in the most. The one who I asked for advice from all the time. The one I shared those deep dark secrets with that I knew no one else would understand.

I pulled out the envelope and broke the seal. My hands were shaking, not ready to read what her final words to me were going to be. I can only imagine the fear she was feeling, knowing that one day we might all be reading these letters. What do you say to someone to help them get over such a great loss?

Becca,

First off, please don't be mad at me. I know that if you are reading this that I am gone and that means that you have seen Ethan. If you haven't seen him yet because you read this before my funeral then you have to promise me that you will still go. You cannot deny me that.

I figured that you would wait to read this, that you would put it off as long as possible. (I hope I'm right or else you are going to be real mad at me for planning all of this before I died.) Just remember that everything I am doing, I am doing out of love for you, Morgan, for everyone.

Listen, I know that things are going to be difficult for you, for Morgan, for my family, for a number of people. I was awesome and everyone knew it. :) J/K You will all get through this. You will need to lean on each other, to hold each other up from time to time, but you will all get through this. I need for you to get through this because the thought of leaving all of you is hard enough on me. I need for you to remember the good times and keep my memory alive. Promise? Good.

So, I don't know how I can say this without making you angry at a dead person (me) but I am going to try. Feel free to not speak to me (or my grave) for a few weeks if you don't like what I have to say. I'll still be looking down on you, watching and protecting that humungous heart of yours. Because it is, larger than you are even aware.

Ethan loves you. You know this, I know this and he knows this. It's not much of a secret to the rest of our friends either. You two need to talk. You need to lay out all your cards and tell him how you feel. I know that just the thought of being alone in a room with him scares you but if I didn't think that it would solve all your problems then I wouldn't be recommending it. Don't waste any more time not being together. Life is way too short for that.

Your package is still sitting where I left it, probably. I don't remember much from the day this all started, but I do remember taking your delivery, sending you that text and leaving it by the couch. Knowing Morgan, he hasn't moved a thing in the house since I came to the hospital.

Morgan. I don't even know what to say about him. He is my soul mate, like Ethan is yours. He is the best thing that ever happened to me and this is going to destroy his beautiful spirit for a while. I need for you to take care of him, to help him through this, to make sure that he moves on. I want him to lead a full life. I want him to find someone to spend his life with, to marry, to have children and grow old with. That was supposed to be me, but I'm not going to be available to take the job. I need for you to make sure that this happens.

As for Brad, please don't be mad at him either. I know that he has always had your best interests at heart and the fact that I made him call and tell Ethan that I was gone was not his choice. I made him do it because I knew that he could handle it, and I couldn't let him go on pretending any more. You two are the best of friends, you make the best of friends, but you SUCK as a couple, and you are not meant to be a couple. I think you both know it and that you're both scared to admit it to each other. Just be friends and nothing more. You can't say that you never tried...it just didn't work out. Be his friend and let him be yours. You both need a friend right now.

I don't want to say good-bye because the thought of that sucks. The only thing I know that I can say is that I love you. You are a wonderful friend, you always have been. I'm so happy that you moved here and that we were given the opportunity to meet. Thank your mom for me (and give her a hug). I will see you again someday (hopefully not soon), and we will pick right back up where we left off, at a coffee shop in heaven.

Until then...Natalie

Oh! My! God! The letter floats to the floor before I even realize that I've let it go. I reach for it but the tears won't stop coming, and I can't seem to focus enough to find it on the floor. I hate her right now. She couldn't have made me laugh or cry more, and she's not even here to yell at. *Crap! Crap! Crap!* How does she even know what to say to me right now? How did she pick the very right words? How is she still so inside my head when I can only feel her presence in my heart?

I hear the door creak and when I look up, I'm staring into the most gorgeous, emerald green eyes I have even seen. Of all the people to walk in on me when I'm such a mess, to walk in on me at the worst moment imaginable, it would have to be him. That's when I realized that he's not alone. Brad's right behind him. *Crap!*

"Can we come in?"

It's a rhetorical question, of course, because Ethan's halfway in the bathroom already as he's asking. Brad's standing just outside the door, and I am starting to feel a little trapped. I don't really have much of a choice in the matter.

I nod twice, and Brad moves in and closes the door behind him. I stand and turn my back to both of them. Looking in the mirror, I try my best to fix my makeup and wash away the tear stains on my cheeks. I can feel them staring at me, and I am doing my best to avoid making eye contact in the mirror. The bathroom isn't exactly small, but I am starting to feel claustrophobic.

Ethan disappears from view, and I hear the crinkle of paper close behind me. I turn quickly and snatch the letter out of his hand. I do my best to fold it back up, and I shove it in the envelope on the counter and then back into my purse. The last thing I need is for either one of them to read what she wrote to me. At least, not right now.

"Was that the letter Natalie wrote you?" I'm staring right into Ethan's eyes as Brad speaks. I want to be polite and look at him as I respond, but I can't tear my eyes away. It's like I'm in a trance or something. I nod to let him know that it was, and finally close my eyes to break the spell.

"Yeah. Did you get one too? Either of you?"

"We both did. Brad's had specific instruction to call me and let me know she had passed. Mine had specific instruction to read her letter at the funeral. There was some other stuff in the letter, I'm sure in Brad's too. What did she want you to do?"

"She wants me to take care of Morgan. She wants me to make sure he moves on with his life and doesn't let her loss consume him. She wants me to move on with my life…" I have to pause. How am I going to say this to the both of them right now. It's not the right time, but it may be the only time I have them in the same room together. Why are they together? Aren't they supposed to hate each other? "Wait. Why are you two here, together?"

"Everyone's here. The luncheon started a few minutes ago, and everyone's starting to arrive. We were looking for you." Brad's answer seemed so simple. A couple of friends looking for another friend at a "party." Problem with that scenario is that they are not supposed to be friends.

"Together? You were looking for me together? Why? You hate each other."

"Hate is a strong word, Becca. We've found a way to move past all that and to coexist." Really, Ethan? Coexist? You don't even live on the same continent. That makes it pretty easy to coexist.

This is too weird. I need to get out of this bathroom. I need to get away from the both of them and clear my mind. Everything Natalie wrote is too fresh. The wounds that I've worked so hard to close, to stitch up and move on from, are opening again. I can literally feel my heart cracking in my chest and there's nothing I can do to avoid what's about to happen. I need air, fresh air. I need to be alone, to get away.

"Okay. So you coexist now. Great. I'm happy for you, both of you. I however cannot coexist with both of you at the same time. I just can't. So, I need to go. I have some setup to do still. I have to help the caterers and stuff."

I try to push past Ethan but he doesn't budge. I'm trapped. I try again but he's solid as a rock. His muscles are firm. I can feel that he's been working out. I can feel the heat rising from his body, and I know better than to make eye contact with him. I try once more to move past him but it's useless. He's not budging, and I don't have the strength or the willpower to fight him.

Unglued

"Brad. Can you give us a few minutes? We'll meet you downstairs."

I can feel his stare, but I still avoid making eye contact. He's taking charge of the situation. I can feel his dominance surround me. It's a new feeling, but somehow still familiar. It reminds me of the first time we met. It reminds me of how drawn to him I once was, or still am. It reminds me of how much trouble we could get into if Brad were to actually leave us alone in the bathroom right now.

Click. Without saying a word, Brad's gone. The sound of the lock sliding into place, the scraping of the metal, to ensure our privacy is the only sound in the bathroom right now. Now, I not only feel trapped, I am trapped. I can feel my heart starting to race, my breathing is picking up speed. It's so hot in here. I feel faint. I retreat to the toilet and take a seat.

Ethan loves you. You know this, I know this and he knows this. It's not much of a secret to the rest of our friends either. You two need to talk.

I can almost hear Natalie speaking to me. The sound of her voice fills my ears. Her laughter. The serious tone that she used to take with me when it came to Ethan. The way she used to attempt to make a joke at the worst moments just to make me smile. I can hear her voice so clearly.

I close my eyes in an attempt to shut her out but there she is, standing in front of me. Her smile is so bright. I can feel the tears running down my face, but all I can focus on is the sight of my best friend standing in front of me. She's waving her finger at me, and the look on her face tells me that she's not pleased with me.

He loves you, Becca. Listen to what he has to say. You need each other right now. You need to move past so much that you'll never be able to do that unless you talk. So talk to him, Becca. Tell him how you feel. Tell him how much you love him, how much you miss him and how much you still want to be with him. He needs to hear it as much as you do. Just talk to him. You can do it, Becca. Just breathe. Breathe and talk. For me...

She's gone. Just like that, she's gone. One second she's in front of me, pushing me to do what needs to be done, scolding me for being so scared. The next second she's faded away, and I'm staring up at the ceiling. Then Ethan's face comes into view.

Crap!

"Is it just me or do you faint on everyone?"

I fainted. I fainted from fear. I fainted in front of Ethan, again. Good gravy, what is wrong with me? *Just breathe. Breathe and talk.*

Damn her! Even after she's gone and left me, she's still telling me what to do. She's right, but that's beside the point.

"I'm sorry. I don't know what happened. I got really hot and then… well, let's not rehash that. Why? Why are we in here, Ethan?"

"I think we both know that we need to talk. I'm sure Brad's right outside. If you feel more comfortable, I can always ask him to come back in."

"No. I'm fine. I just don't understand why this can't wait. Why today? I have enough to deal with today. I'm not sure if I can handle anything else."

"Do you think you can at least listen to what I have to say?"

"I suppose I can try." I don't really think I can handle it. Can I tell him that?

"I'm gonna lay it all out there, Becca. It's gonna be a lot to hear and I know that it's gonna be hard, but I really need you to just listen. I want you to hear every word that I say. I want you to absorb it all. When I'm done, well, we can go from there. Can you do that for me?"

No. That's what I wanted to say, but I once again have lost my ability to speak. His voice has hit deep, causing my body to react. I try to ignore it, but his presence has become so overwhelming. I nod once for him to continue, but before he does, he helps me back up onto the toilet. He turns his back to me as if what he has to say is too hard to do if he's looking at me. This is going to suck big time!

"Okay, I don't really know where to begin. I guess I should start with I'm sorry. I overreacted to what happened. I was frustrated and scared and thought I was losing you, so I decided that I would be the one to leave. I was too proud to let you leave me I guess. It was a mistake. My biggest mistake to date, but I know that there is no taking it back."

He pauses like he's allowing it to sink in a minute before continuing. I hear something, and I think it's him whispering something but I realize that it's him crying, or attempting not to. Without thinking, I move to his side and intertwine our fingers.

He turns. Our bodies are inches apart, and I look up to avoid staring directly at his chest. Big mistake! I make eye contact and that's all it took. I felt my back hit the wall, and I probably should have cried out in pain, but I was not thinking clearly. I was not thinking at all. My body had taken over for my brain and was now in charge.

His lips hit mine at the same moment he lifted me by the thighs so that I could wrap my legs around his waist. It was all happening so fast that before I knew it, I was missing my underwear, and his pants were on the floor. I cried out the moment our bodies connected from the pure sense of pleasure.

It had been so long. Ethan is the only man I have ever been with. I figured that at some point in time that Brad would want to move our relationship forward, and that I would decide at that point if I was ready for the physical part. He never tried to move our relationship in that direction, and I didn't push him to. Why hadn't I pushed?

"Oh, Becca. I've missed you so much."

I want to respond, to tell him how much I've missed him as well but I can't seem to find my voice. I think the little noises that I was making were saying enough at that point anyway.

When it was over, and our bodies separated, I felt empty. For those few moment, I was not thinking about losing Natalie or about how I lost Ethan. For those few moments, I didn't have to think at all. All I had to do was feel. Now that I was focused on feeling, all I felt was empty and lost.

"I'm sorry. I don't know what came over me. That's not exactly the direction I planned our conversation would go."

"It's fine. It's not like I didn't consent."

"Did I hurt you?" After he said it, he realized how it sounded. Did you hurt me now or did you hurt me before? Am I still hurting? "I'm sorry."

"Stop apologizing. I knew what was happening and I allowed it to continue. I'm just as much at fault as you are for what just happened. Just, stop apologizing. It makes me feel like it was a mistake." I'm lashing out at him to cover the way I'm really feeling and I know it.

"Okay. I'm…Anyway. Can we finish talking now?"

"I think I've had about as much as I can handle for one day. I need to get downstairs. Actually, I just need to be alone right now."

"Okay. Can I call you then? Tomorrow?"

"No. When I'm ready to talk, I'll call you."

I didn't give him a chance to respond. I reached past him and unlocked the door. He knew that I was done for right now. He moved to the side so that I could pass. I closed the door behind me and made my way down the stairs as gracefully as I could. My legs were sore. My

back was sore. My whole body was sore.
 Crap!
 My underwear! I never put them back on.

Chapter Sixteen

I waited three days before I picked up my phone and attempted to dial Ethan's number. I hung up twice before pressing send. On my third attempt, I hit Send and then hung up before it started ringing. I took that as my sign that I still wasn't ready to talk to him.

Our talk was inevitable. It had to take place and it had to take place soon. Ethan had to head back to England, eventually. I never asked him when he was leaving. In order to ask him, I would actually have to call him. I would actually have to speak with him. I would have to make sure that I found my voice in his presence. It keeps disappearing whenever he is around.

Today was the day that I was going to get my life back on track. A fresh start. A new beginning. I was going back to school today, back to work, and leaving my house for the first time since Natalie's funeral. I was getting my life back on track, or so I thought.

I grabbed my bag, slung it over my shoulder, and headed out to my car. I went to toss it in the backseat when something caught my eye. *Crap!* I never took my package from Ethan out of my car.

It's not heavy, but I walk slowly and carry it with both hands just to make sure that I don't drop it. I make it up to my room and stand in the doorway wondering what to do with it. It's still wrapped. I have no intentions of hanging it on the wall as a constant reminder of the day my life fell apart.

I settle for the closet, keeping it wrapped for now. One day, I will unwrap it and put everything behind me. Today is not going to be that day.

I open my closet and slide it against the right wall. I can feel that it doesn't want to go, but I continue to shove it until I am finally tired of pushing. I get down on my knees and start moving stuff out of the way. Shoes, clothes, more shoes. My favorite pair of sandals. I've been looking for those for a while now.

My tennis bag, the one Ethan got me. How ironic. Of all the things that could potentially be blocking my way and it had to be that bag, from that person. This is a sign. It has to be. The package from Ethan. The tennis bag from Ethan. All of it is pointing me toward him. I need to call him, to talk to him even though I'm scared.

I knew if I opened the bag that I would find two racquets, probably a dozen balls, and some ankle wrap. It was all I used to keep in there on a permanent basis. I want to open it, to pull everything out, and throw it against the wall. More than anything, I want to put the bag high on my shoulder and take it with me. I want to hit some balls against the practice wall and forget everything that's happened for just a few minutes. I want to zone out like I used to when I would practice. I need it.

I pull the bag out of the closet completely and slide the package in. I toss everything back in, minus my sandals and the tennis bag, and close the door. I quickly swap out my shoes for the sandals and toss the discarded ones in my tennis bag for later. There was no way I would be able to play in these shoes, no matter how cute they are.

I'm out the door, tennis bag in hand, and on my way to class. I'm officially five minutes late. I need to get lucky, find a close spot and run to class if I was going to make it on time. Who was I kidding? There was no way I was running in these shoes, and there was no way I was getting lucky enough to find a close parking spot at this time of day. I was going to be late, no matter what.

I hit every light, found a close parking spot, and speed walked to class. I was still late. My saving grace today was our professor. Apparently, the copy machine had jammed with our test in it, and he was waiting for it to be fixed. My lucky day!

I had almost two hours between the end of class and the start of my shift at the coffee shop. This is when I normally went to see Natalie.

There was no point in driving home to turn around and drive right back. The hospital was close and seeing Natalie became a part of my routine. Today, I needed to start a new routine.

I walked to my car and changed my shoes. I grabbed my bag and headed over to the tennis courts. I knew that there was a chance that I would run into a former teammate or any number of people. I was willing to take that chance today. I needed to do this, for myself.

One year, four months, and three days. That's the amount of time it's been since I stepped on this court with a racquet in my hands. That's the amount of time it's been since I picked up a racquet. That's the amount of time it's been since I hit a ball. One year, four months, and three days.

I stood outside the gates for a while before I finally found the strength to step inside. The courts were empty. I didn't even see any students passing by. I felt a pair of eyes on me, the presence of another person. I scanned the area, but I didn't see anyone.

I dropped my bag and sat down next to it. If I learned anything from my accident, it was to stretch before playing. I may not have been competing today, or any day soon, but I knew that I still needed to stretch my muscles before I even thought about picking up a racquet.

It felt good to stretch. It had been way too long since I had taken the time to use some of the muscles I was about to use. I was scared. I knew that things would not work like they used to. I knew that I would never be as good as I used to be. The doctors said that I would never be able to play again. At least not competitively.

I never tried. I gave up without trying. I knew that I would have to work hard to come back from my injury, but I let the doctors decide my fate. They would not sign off on my release to play without me proving to them that I was able to play without being in pain, without damaging my shoulder further.

The pain. I was about to cause myself pain for the first time in a long time. I pulled my arm across my chest and stretched the muscles in my shoulder. They were extremely tight. I had managed to overcome most of the challenges I had had in the beginning. Was this worth it? Did I really need to play?

I needed something. I needed something back in my life. So much had been taken from me in the past year. So many people, and the only thing I truly loved beyond control, tennis. This was the one thing that I knew I could get back. I needed this.

I hop to my feet, trying to find the strength to reach in my bag and pull out a racquet. They were probably in need of restringing, or at least the strings needed to be tightened. That was the least of my concerns right now. Right now, all I could focus on was the fact that I was going to do this, that I needed to do this, that I wanted to do this.

With my racquet in one hand and two balls in the other, I slowly approached the practice wall. It's not much, two very large pieces of plywood attached to the fencing, but I knew every square inch of that wall at one point in time and could predict exactly where the ball would go. Now, it looked like two very large pieces of plywood that were as unpredictable as I was. It scared me, plain and simple.

Some people say the first step to recovery is the hardest. For me, the first step was admitting that I was injured, beyond repair, beyond my control. I gave up control. I gave up tennis in hopes that it would help me move on with the rest of my life. For me, the first step was not the hardest, it was the easiest.

Coming back here, picking up a racquet and attempting to play again…this is going to be the hardest step for me. It's not step one but it's not the last step in the process for me either. Today is going to go one of two ways for me. Either I will be able to handle this, physically and emotionally, or I won't be able to.

Time to find out. Time to take my first swing and see which way this was going to turn out. Time to see how strong I am. My physical and mental strength are both in question, and I need to know how strong I am. For me. For my sanity.

I give the ball a bounce. Once. Twice. It still feels natural. The time that's elapsed since the last time I even held a ball is gone. Everything around me is gone. It's me and the ball and nothing else right now.

One more bounce and I find myself swinging. The ball sails towards the boards and back towards me just as quickly. I'm not ready for it and I swing late, missing the ball completely.

My determination is overwhelming. I can feel my sense of pride bubbling over. I will hit the ball. I will not let one miss determine my abilities.

Bounce.
Bounce.
Swing.

It sails towards the boards and bounces back toward me. This time, I'm ready. I swing and my racquet connects. The ball sails back toward the boards again and then back toward me. I connect a second time, but my swing was a little too early. I was a little too eager. The racquet connects and sends the ball sailing over the left side of the boards and outside the court.

I walk with determination to where my ball has landed outside the courts. That's when I feel it again. I can feel someone watching me again. My body shudders as I bend down to pick up my ball. I glance around as I make my way back to the court, but I don't spot anyone. Am I going crazy?

After playing in front of crowds for years, I am starting to feel self-conscious. Never once did I feel anyone watching me. Except Ethan. I always knew when he was close, when he was watching. I could feel him then and I can feel him now. He was close, too close.

I close the gate behind me and approach the practice boards again. I feel the first drop as I bounce the ball. I look up to the sky and it's clear, perfectly clear. I am going crazy. I feel another drop and this time I ignore it.

It's the middle of July. Monsoon season is approaching, but we have yet to have our first massive rainfall. All the washes are dry and there have been no reports of rain yet. There was no way it was going to rain today.

I hit the ball and it comes back to me quickly, but I'm ready. My timing is perfect. I hit it back to the boards and it comes right back to me. I'm starting to feel comfortable after it comes back a third time and try my backhand.

The moment I reach across my body and pull the racquet back, I instantly regret my decision. The pain starts in my shoulder and travels down to my hand. I drop my racquet before the ball even reaches me. I grab my shoulder and a silent scream escapes my lips.

The pain is so intense that I drop to my knees. I'm holding my shoulder with my left hand and trying to rub the pain away, but it's only making it worse. I know that I'm done for the day, but I don't want to admit it to myself just yet. I want to keep going, to push through the pain, but I can't even manage to stand up.

Then the rain comes. It's not a light shower. There is no warning, no preface to the massive storm that's coming from the fluffy white clouds above. The rain is coming down hard and fast. I'm soaked to the bone and can barely see two feet in front of me. I need to stand up and gather my things. I need to get out of the rain and to my car as quickly as possible.

I feel a set of hands pull me up by my waist. I don't need to turn around to know who's standing behind me. I can feel his presence. My heart rate has sped up, and my body betrays me by shuddering the second he touches my shoulder.

I turned to see him standing only inches from me. His shirt is soaked, plastered to his chest, and I can see his nipple ring. I want to reach out and touch it. It's almost like his body is calling to me. It wants to be touched. It wants me to tug on it.

I averted my eyes to the court below my feet. What do I say to him? Why is he even here? No one knew I was coming here today. I didn't even know that I was coming here today. How did he find me?

"Why don't we get out of the rain? You're shivering."

"I'm fine. I actually need to get to work."

There was so much more I wanted to say, so much I wanted to ask him. I chickened out. I reached down and grabbed my racquet with my good arm and walked away. I knew that he was watching me. I knew that he would follow me. I didn't care at that moment. His pull was strong, almost too strong. I needed to get away. I needed distance so I could breathe.

I walked in to work and went straight to the bathrooms. I did my best to ring out my hair and quickly changed into my work clothes. I was officially five minutes late when I finally clocked in. I guess it was my day for being tardy. Luckily, the girl I was replacing was too busy at the moment to notice that I was late.

I took over for her at the counter and tried my best to focus on my job. My thoughts kept drifting back to Ethan, his shirt soaked, and his nipple ring taunting me. By the time I turned the sign to Closed and started to clean up, I was mentally exhausted. My shoulder was killing me, and all I wanted was to go to bed.

I was in the back filling my mop bucket when I heard the front door chime. I instantly went on alert. I thought I had locked the door, but I don't remember actually doing it. Someone was inside. Someone let themselves in, and I was the only one here. I needed something to protect myself. I needed a weapon.

I went into the office and grabbed a pair of scissors. I knew that they wouldn't scare anyone away, but they would hopefully be able to cause enough pain to allow me to escape. There was only one way in and one way out of the coffee shop, and the intruder was between me and the exit.

I heard someone say hello. I heard someone call my name. They knew I was here, there was no use hiding. They knew who I was. I grabbed the scissors and put them in my back pocket. If nothing else, I would have them if I needed them.

I peeked around the corner and into the cafe. I instantly froze. What was he doing here?

He scared the crap out of me. I couldn't believe that he had the nerve to come into the café knowing that I would be by myself and knowing we were closed. What kind of idiot does that to a person, especially someone they are supposed to care about?

"What are you doing here?"

"I just wanted to check on you and see how your shoulder was feeling. You looked like you were in quite a bit of pain earlier and I wanted to check on you."

Of course he would show up here. There was no escaping him. I knew that we needed to talk, it was evident, and he was being quite persistent. Following me around was not making me want to talk to him more. It was actually making me want to talk to him less. His constant presence was making me scared. Scared of what I was feeling, scared of what I still felt for him, and scared of finding out if he felt the same way.

"I'm fine. I told you that earlier." I was being cold. I knew it, but there was no stopping it. I was trying to save myself from heartache again. I wouldn't survive losing him again.

"I know. You're fine. Anytime I ask you how you are, you say that you're fine. Why not try telling me the truth for a change. How are you, Becca?"

"I'm…What do you really want, Ethan? I know this is not about my shoulder. You watched me play today. You were there. Now you're here. What do you want?"

"You. That's all I want. I want you back in my life. I want things to go back to the way they were before I messed them up. I want us again."

That was what I was afraid of. I felt the same way, but I knew that if I gave in, that he could hurt me again. Self-preservation.

"I don't know if I can give you that. After you left, I fell apart. It took me a long time to pull myself back up, and I can't go through that again. I won't be able to recover this time. Natalie…well, she was a large part of my recovery. She helped me out of a very dark place, and she's not here to save me if that happens again."

I barely got the last part out. I hadn't said Natalie's name since her funeral. I hadn't allowed myself to really let it sink in that she wasn't here anymore. I had read and re-read her letter every day, more than once a day, since her funeral. The pain was still present and her words were still fresh.

Don't waste any more time not being together. Life is way too short for that.

"I can't promise you that I won't hurt you again, or that it won't be hard, but do you know what I can promise you?"

I knew it was a trick question. Promises were made to be broken. No one can promise anyone anything and know that they will be able to keep that promise. I wanted to hear this, though.

"What? What is it that you think you can promise me and keep?"

"To love you. I promise to love you until the day I die. I've loved you since the moment I laid eyes on you, and I've never stopped loving you. The moment I left was the worst moment of my life. I was angry and sad and confused, but I still loved you. I loved you then, I love you now, and I've loved you every moment in-between. That's what I can promise you, that's all I can promise you."

Wow! That's all? I want to tell him that I love him too, that I've never stopped loving him. I want to tell him that every moment we've spent apart, every second of every hour of every day, I spent loving him because I don't know how to not love him. That's what I want to say.

"Oh."

I am once again speechless. My voice is absent and in its place is a bewildered expression and an empty shell of a person who is trying to become whole again, one step at a time. His words fill my heart, and all of a sudden my feet are moving my body in his direction.

I stop just short of where he's standing. I can see that his breathing is as labored as mine. Standing this close to him is making my knees weak and my pulse race. My heart is beating loudly in my chest, and for a moment, I think that I might faint again.

I close my eyes and just breathe. I need to breathe. Once again, his presence is making my head swim. His presence is all I feel and it's beyond overwhelming. I want him to wrap his arms around me, to hold me, and to tell me that this will really work. That everything will be okay. That no matter what, things will work out. That's what I want him to tell me, but I know that it won't be okay, no matter what kind of promises he makes me.

"I believe you. I believe that you would never intentionally hurt me again. I believe that you still love me, that you will always love me. I believe you, but you broke my heart. You broke it into a million pieces the day you left, and I still haven't found a way to piece it back together. I wouldn't survive if you broke it again. I wouldn't know how to move on, to live. I want to give you my heart, I really do, but I can't. It's still shattered."

He's speechless. I knew that as hard as it was for me to hear that he still loved me, that it would be harder for him to hear that I was still hurt. Was I still in love with him? Absolutely! That didn't change the fact that I was still broken and scared. That didn't change the fact that I was unsure of everything involving him. That didn't change the fact that I needed to guard my heart and that was what I was doing. I was guarding my heart.

"I leave tomorrow night. I have to get back to work, and I don't want to leave things between us like this. I thought…well, I thought that maybe we could try again."

I could hear the disappointment in his voice. I saw it in the way his shoulder slumped forward and his head bowed towards the floor. I felt awful, but I knew that this was it, the way it had to be. There was no other option.

"I'm sorry, really. I don't know what else to say."

"Me too."

He turned to walk away but paused when he got to the door. I knew what he was going to say even before he spoke. I felt the same way. It was the end.

"I love you, Becca. I always will."

I closed my eyes and felt the tears running down my cheeks. The door chimed and when I opened my eyes, he was gone. I was wrong. I thought that by keeping him at a distance, by shutting him out, that I was protecting my heart. I thought that if I let him go that I wouldn't feel the pain. Opening my eyes to find that he wasn't standing there anymore,broke my heart all over again.

Chapter Seventeen

"I can't believe you let him go. Why? You still love him don't you?"
"Of course I still love him. I never stopped loving him."
"Then why didn't you give him another chance?"
"I can't."
"Why, Becca?"
"It hurts. It hurts so much."
"What hurts?"
"My heart. It hurts without him. It hurts when I'm around him."
"That's not pain, at least not the kind of pain you think it is."
"What do you mean it's not pain? It hurts!"
"Your heart doesn't hurt, Becca. Your heart yearns. When he's not around it yearns for him. When he is around it yearns for him. Your heart wants what you're denying it. It wants Ethan. It belongs to Ethan."
"That doesn't even make sense. How can my heart want him after what happened. He broke my heart, Natalie. He destroyed me."
"The heart wants what the heart wants. It doesn't have to make sense."
"Why? Why would my heart want him?"
"Think about it. You love him. You love with your heart. Your heart loves him. It's simple. Don't overthink it, Becca."
"It's not about what my heart wants."

Unglued

"Trust me. You need to listen to your heart. It's trying to tell you something."

"What?"

"Listen to your heart, Becca. Listen to your heart."

"But Natalie..."

I awoke with a start. The dream was so real. I was talking to Natalie. She was standing less than five feet away from me. We were sitting at our normal table in the cafeteria. There were people walking around us. I could hear their conversations, the sound of the espresso machine at the coffee stand as it steamed the milk. It was real, too real.

She was arguing with me, debating as she would have said. This can't keep happening. I can't keep dreaming about her, having conversations with her that aren't real. Why is she stalking me in my dreams?

I turned over and my alarm tells me that I have five more minutes before I need to get up. I need a cold shower and a cup of coffee. I need to shake this off. Ethan leaves tonight. Maybe Natalie will leave me alone once he's gone. Knowing her, not a chance.

My shower did little to erase my dream. Everything Natalie had said, in the dream, in her letter, was the only thing I could think about as I was getting ready. I heard my mom come in from work and head into her room to go to sleep. I thought about going in and talking to her, asking her for her opinion, but stopped myself once I realized that I would have to tell her about my dream, about talking to Natalie. I would sound crazy and I knew it.

I heard the coffee machine beep, letting me know that it had finished brewing. Just the thought of a cup of coffee put a pep in my step. I quickly finished getting dressed and pulled my hair back in a ponytail. With the heat and possible storm headed our way, there was no point trying to straighten it today. The first drop of rain would cause instant frizz.

I bounced down the stairs with a sense of purpose, but stopped dead in my tracks when I saw Brad waiting for me in the kitchen. He was leaning against the counter with a steaming cup of coffee in one hand and what looked like a letter in the other. My eyes were drawn to the letter when I saw the handwriting on the front.

Natalie.

I knew that I was not the only one who had gotten a letter. She had written one to Ethan, Morgan, her parents, and Brad as well. She may have written more than just that, but no one else had said anything.

His smile was tentative as best. It barely reached his eyes and his body language told me that whatever was about to happen, I was not going to like it.

"Morning."

"Hey. What are you doing here?"

"I came for the coffee."

"Right. So, why are you really here because we both know I make my coffee strong and you take it weak?"

"You're right. Your coffee is awful. I actually need to talk to you."

The way he said it…I knew. I knew that something was wrong. I knew that whatever we were about to talk about was serious. His posture gave him away. He stood up straight like he was trying to find his confidence, or maybe his inner strength. His smile was gone, and in its place was an expression I've only seen a few times throughout our long relationship.

"Okay. What's up?" I try to sound nonchalant as I make my way around him to the coffee pot. I reach for a mug and slowly fill it with the steaming caffeine that I am in desperate need of right now. I add two spoonful's of sugar and a little creamer before I turn back around to face him.

His expression hasn't changed. He's staring directly at me, and instantly, my knees get weak and my breathing slows. This is bad, really bad.

He slowly hands me the envelope in his hand. I reach out to take it, but before he lets go of it, our eyes meet, and I see in his eyes what I already know in my heart. Our relationship is over.

"Natalie wrote me this. I know she wrote one to you too. She asked me to make sure that you read yours before I had you read mine. I'm not sure what yours said, but I understand why she wants you to read mine."

His hand falls away, and I'm left standing there, holding yet another letter from Natalie. I clutch the letter in my hand and bring it to my chest, over my heart. Why does she want me to read his letter?

"What else, Brad. I know there's something else."

"Read the letter first, Becca, then we can talk. I think it will make more sense that way. As much as I want to disagree with what she wrote, she was right. She was right about a lot of things."

I knew what Natalie had written to me about Brad. I knew she thought that we were better as friends. I was beginning to agree with her, but I figured that Ethan's presence was influencing my perception.

He put his untouched coffee cup down on the counter and moved to stand in front of me. He pulled me into a tight embrace, and I let him hold me. I closed my eyes, and for a moment, I was back in Michigan, on my mom's couch on New Year's Eve, letting him hold me and tell me that everything was going to be okay. My best friend.

He kissed my hair and stepped back. I opened my eyes to find him staring directly at me. The gold specks around his iris twinkling in the light. His eyes were telling me good-bye. He was sad, confused, defeated. I also saw understanding and acceptance. I wasn't losing my best friend, I was getting him back.

"Call me this afternoon, after you read this," he said pointing to the letter in my hand.

I nodded and looked to the floor, breaking our eye contact. I wasn't ready to lose or gain anyone in my life. I was okay with the way things were. I was happy with the way things were. Who was I kidding? Our relationship had never crossed the line beyond friendship, unless you count kissing.

He was gone by the time I looked back up. I hear the front door shut and his car start before I even attempted to move. I looked up at the clock to see that I had to leave for class. I pulled out a travel mug and transferred my coffee. I was going to need it if I was going to make it through this day. I shove Natalie's letter in my bag, and I'm out the door in less than two minutes.

Class was less than entertaining. I was focused on the letter in my bag the entire time, and the professor's lecture barely registered on my radar. I was distracted. Even after trying to clear my mind and focus, I knew I still wasn't going to retain any of the lecture.

After class, I went and got a refill on my coffee then sought out a quiet spot to read Natalie's letter. I walked around looking for the perfect place and ended up at the tennis courts. They were empty again surprisingly.

My tennis bag was in the backseat of my car where I left it the other day. I contemplated walking back across campus to where I had parked but knew that if I did, I would not get this letter read.

I opened the gate and headed towards the practice boards. I plopped down on the court and rested my back against the boards. It took me a minute to find the letter in my bag. Once it was in my hand, it was like my heart jumpstarted itself.

I knew I had to get this over with. I knew that whatever Natalie had written was obviously important to her. She must have felt that in some way, her knowledge, her opinion, would somehow help. I had no doubt that it would, but I was scared to see what she had written to Brad. If it was anything like what she had written to me, I could only imagine the heartbreak he was feeling right now.

Brad,

I know that this letter is unexpected but I want you to know that I have always considered you a close friend. I may not have always agreed with your methods or your relationship with Becca, but I always understood how important she was to you and how much you care about her.

That's why I need for you to do a few things for me. Call me selfish and bossy but I really think that it's for the best, for both of you. I know that you love her but I think you love her the only way that you know how, the only way that you ever have. She's your best friend. She's your other half. That's the way things were meant to be. You two were meant to be friends. I know that a lot of people say that the best relationships develop from friendship. I agree with that, wholeheartedly. I don't think any relationship is as strong unless you are also friends with the person you love, that you respect them for who they are, and that you accept them unconditionally. You two have all of that but you are missing the one key component to having a successful relationship.

You have to be the one that owns her heart, Brad, and unfortunately for you, her heart belongs to Ethan. I know that you two have fought for her, over her, but I think it's time for Becca to finally decide what she wants, who she wants to be with. In the letter I wrote her, I told her to let you go. I am not trying to hurt you by telling you that. Whether she listens to me or not is up to her. I know she loves you, deeply, but I also know that if she was "in love" with you that your relationship would have progressed by now.

Like I said, I'm not telling you this to hurt your feelings. I care about you. You are a great friend. I want you to be prepared. Ethan is going to be coming back for my funeral. I'm not trying to be morbid but

Unglued

I know it's inevitable that whatever is wrong with me will eventually be the end of me. I can feel it in my bones. When Ethan comes back, Becca is going to need you. She's going to need someone to help her stand on her own two feet. She's going to need someone to help her through everything—losing me and seeing him again. That person needs to be you.

That brings me to my first favor...I need for you to take care of her for me. I need for you to make sure that she survives this, all of this, and lands on her feet. She's going to need her best friend by her side. I can't be there for her but you can.

Secondly, I need for you to help her forgive Ethan. She forgave herself for what happened, and I know that she never blamed you for anything, but she needs to forgive him. If she can't forgive him, then there will never be any chance that she will find happiness.

Third, I need for you to make sure that Ethan does not leave without the two of them hashing out their relationship. I know this will be hard for you, but I need for you to make sure that this happens, it's important to me, and it will be important to both of them. Once Ethan is gone, assuming Becca is stubborn as usual, I need for you to help her see the light at the end of the tunnel so that she can go after him. She'll let him leave, she'll let him go back to England, and then she'll regret it. Help her see the light so that she goes to England and makes amends with him. The only catch here is that she won't do that if she's still dating you. She's going to need you for this but she's not going to need her boyfriend, she's going to need her best friend.

I will not ask or tell you to break up with her, but I think we both know that in order to uncomplicate her life, being just her friend is what she will need. I'm sorry for that, but I know that you know I'm right.

I'm asking a lot of you and you can't even argue with me or tell me no. I'm sorry, really I am. I know I have the upper hand here but there are still two things I need for you to do for me.

First, I need you to be there for Morgan. Ben is the only real friend he's ever had, and I don't really trust him. His idea of helping Morgan move on will be to take him to a party, get him drunk, and get him laid. If that happens, I will haunt Ben for the rest of his life. He's going to need a shoulder to lean on, someone to help him pick up the pieces and build a new puzzle. He's going to take this the hardest. He's just going to need friends, and you and Becca are the only ones I trust.

Secondly, I need for you to call Ethan. Let him know that I'm gone. Let him know when the funeral is so that he can be here. I have sent him a letter and asked him to do something for me, but he needs to know that I'm gone. I would do this myself but…well, I guess that's a bad joke. I've never really been able to tell a good one, and I shouldn't try to start now.

Take care of her and take care of yourself, Brad. Everyone will survive without me. They will be sad but they will move on. Life goes on. I just won't be there to make it interesting.

Natalie

I'm crying. I know I'm crying, but I don't really know why. Natalie knew what would happen. She knew that I would fall apart, that I would need someone to lean on, that I would send Ethan away even though my heart was conflicted about it. She knew everything. It's almost like she set all of this in motion, but why?

I no longer wondered why Brad wanted me to read his letter first. It explained a lot. How Ethan knew about Natalie. Why he came back to town. Mostly, it explained what I knew he wanted to talk to me about. He was going to break up with me, and as much as I knew that it was supposed to hurt, it just didn't.

I immediately picked up my phone to call him. There was no use wasting time. I unlocked my screen to find two new text messages waiting for me. One was from my boss and one was from Ethan. Oh boy! Here we go.

I overscheduled today so I don't need you to come in. Call George is you really want to work. He may give up his shift.

No, thank you. I will gladly take the night off.

Ethan: I leave at 7. I still think we need to talk. Call me please.

Again, no thank you. I can't deal with that right now. Right now, my boyfriend is about to break up with me and that is enough drama and heartache for one day. A girl can only take so much.

Instead of calling Brad, I sent him a quick text telling him to meet me at my house. I don't want to do this over the phone. I feel I, at least, deserve a face to face with him if he's going to go through with it. I'm not debating the fact that I think Natalie is right, there's no one to debate it with.

I headed back to my car and cranked the air. It's hot out today. I'm covered in sweat from sitting on the courts, soaking up the sun. I can feel the heat on my cheeks. The cold air is refreshingly blowing on my face, and for a moment, I closed my eyes and let the cooling feeling take over.

A short moment turned into a half hour. I woke up to the sound of my phone alerting me to a new text. I hadn't realized I had fallen asleep. I hadn't realized that I was even tired. Apparently, the sun had taken more out of me than I thought.

Brad: Are you on your way? I'm getting worried about you.

He was waiting for me at my house.

I fastened my seatbelt and put my car in reverse. I know what will happen when I get there. I know what to expect. Still, I'm nervous. I don't want to lose my friend, my confidant. I don't want to lose him completely. I knew it might happen if we started dating, but I wasn't thinking about it at the time.

At the time, all I wanted was to feel loved by someone. To share my life with someone. Someone to hold me at night and talk to during the day. In hindsight, I had all of that with Brad as my friend. I didn't need to risk everything.

The drive feels like it takes forever and not long enough at the same time. One minute I'm waiting for the light on campus to change, and the next I'm turning onto my street. I remember passing work. I remember passing my turn that would have taken me to Natalie's house.

I pull in the driveway, and my heart feels like it's about to jump out of my chest. I can hear it beating over my radio. I can feel the pounding against my skin. I'm not sure why I'm nervous, anxious. I'm not sure what I'm expecting to happen.

I see him waiting for me in the living room as I dropped my bag by the stairs. I contemplated going up, taking a moment and composing myself, but I'm still not sure what's about to happen. I need to be strong. I know Natalie would want me to face this, head on, and move forward with my life after all is said and done. I tried to do that with Ethan, and

I was unsuccessful. I have the chance to redeem myself right now, and I needed to take that chance.

"Hey."

"Hey. It's about time. I was starting to get worried about you. The storm is going to be here in about fifteen minutes, and I didn't want you out driving around in it."

"I'm fine. I fell asleep in my car."

"Okay. So, did you read Natalie's letter?"

Nothing like getting straight to the point.

"Yeah."

"Okay. I need to say some things before we talk about it. I know you are wondering why I asked you to read it."

"Yeah. I understand that Natalie's opinion mattered to you, to me, but I don't understand why you wanted me to read her letter."

"Trust me. After I'm done saying what I have to say, you will understand."

"I trust you, completely. You should know that by now."

"Good." He pauses and takes a deep breath. I know that this is going to be hard to hear, but I have a feeling that it's going to be harder for him to say. "I love you, more than anything else in this world. Natalie helped me realize that. After Ethan left… well, you weren't the only person that was in a dark place. I felt responsible. I felt awful about everything. I was selfish and wasn't thinking about anyone else but myself and how I felt, what I wanted. Natalie pushed me to talk about my feelings, about how I felt about you. She knew that I loved you, that I was in love with you, and she helped me see that what I did was not malicious. It was out of love. I reached for what I wanted and took a chance."

The tears at the corners of his eyes caused me to look away. I can't bear to see him cry. If he does, I will start, and right now I am being strong. I have to keep reminding myself of that.

"I didn't realize until it was too late that what I was feeling was jealousy. Yes, I love you. I always have. I always will. What I was feeling when I kissed you in the bathroom that day was not love. It was me wanting something that I knew I couldn't have and trying to take it with no thought about the consequences. I was selfish."

To hear him say it is unreal. It's amazing how when things are put into perspective, the light shines down and the answers are clear.

"After talking to Natalie and Morgan and then Ethan I knew…"

"You talked to Ethan? About what happened?"

"Yes, I'm getting to that. At first, we both just yelled, a lot. Once we calmed down enough to have a civilized conversation, we worked things out. I took the blame, and we made amends. He's still not my biggest fan, but we called a truce and both decided that we needed to focus on your happiness and not our own. If you're happy, we will be happy. We both love you and that's really all that matters in the end."

"So, the two of you decided what was best for me, without asking me what I wanted?" I can hear the anger in my voice so I'm sure that he can hear it too.

"Yes. But listen. He's still in love with you. He wants to be with you, for things to go back to the way they were. So do I. You were happy then. You were the happiest I have ever seen you when you and Ethan were together. You need that happiness in your life right now. So I am bowing out gracefully. I will always be here for you, always be a part of your life, and always love you more than I will ever be able to put into words. And I know you love me too, but not like you love him. I am your best friend, I always will be, and right now, you need a friend. You need a shoulder to cry on. You need us, the old version of us. Let me be that person for you again, Becca."

I don't really know what to say. He's giving me a choice. I have to make the decision, and I don't know what the right answer is. I'm mad at him for talking to Ethan. I'm mad at Ethan for keeping tabs on me behind my back. I'm mad at Natalie for making us have this conversation. Most of all, I'm mad at myself for causing all of this. In the end, it really was my fault that I was even in this predicament. I was the one who caused this.

I heard the rain starting to fall outside. The drops hitting the roof of the house made it sound like there was a drum being beat softly from across the room. I closed my eyes and allowed myself a moment of solace and just listened. I'm not sure what I was listening for, but it felt right. I needed for someone to tell me what to say. I needed for someone to tell me the right answers.

I felt it, him. He was either close or he was thinking about me. I knew that deep down inside, I belong to him and he belongs to me. There was no reason to fight it. Brad was right, about everything he was saying. I needed him, my best friend. Without Natalie, he was all I really had, the only one I could really count on. I also needed Ethan. He was the love of my life. I would never love another like I loved him, and I would never feel as loved by another like I feel loved by him.

I opened my eyes to find that Brad was nowhere to be seen. The only evidence that he had even been here was the envelope that was sitting in his place on the couch. I could see my name scribbled across the front of it. It was barely legible beyond the capital B, but I knew it was for me.

I slowly made my way across the room and picked up the envelope. It was from Ethan. His handwriting was unique. I immediately go on alert. I feel him again and this time, the feeling is stronger. I turn, expecting to find him standing behind me, but he's not there. I can see Brad in the kitchen, rummaging through the fridge. The sight brings a smile to my face. He's comfortable, even after the incredibly uncomfortable conversation we just had.

I snuck up behind him and wrapped my arms around his waist. He jumps, unaware of my presence, but immediately relaxes when he realizes it's me. We stand like this, my head resting on his shoulder, my arms wrapped around him tightly, for what feels like forever, but still not long enough. We were breaking up. Our relationship was over, but our friendship was still as strong as ever. It was a good feeling.

"So, are you going to open it, friend?"

"No, friend. I need time before I open it."

"Becca, he leaves in a few hours. You need to open it, sooner rather than later."

I knew he was right but that didn't make it any easier.

"Look, he asked me to make sure that you opened it before he left, but I will leave that up to you. I'm starving and your mom needs to go to the store, so I'm gonna go get some food. I can come back if you want, or I can leave you to do this on your own."

"I got this. I promise to open it as soon as you leave. I think it's time to put an end to all of this."

His smile turned upside down. "I love you to death, but you are delusional."

"Gee, thanks."

"Listen to what you're saying. You want to 'put an end' to all of this. There is only one way this will end, Becca."

"Don't I have a choice in the matter? Don't I get to decide my future? Or did you and Ethan map it out for me already?" I'm instantly angry. Angry at him, at Ethan. I get to decide, not them. I'm a big girl. I can make big girl decisions. I decide what my future holds, no one else.

"Look, I'm not trying to piss you off, but I think you know that your heart has already made its decision. Don't allow your fear to take over."

I want to respond but I can't find the words. My anger has already melted away, and I feel like I want to cry. My emotions are running wild. One minute I feel like the world is crumbling and I want to run and hide, and the next I feel like I'm on top of the world, soaring to the next great thing.

He kisses me on the forehead and turns to leave. He knows that I need to do this alone, but I fear that he also knows what my decision is going to be. How does everyone around me know what is going to happen before I do. It seems very unfair, but life seems unfair right now.

Chapter Eighteen

I grab the letter and my bag and make my way up to my room. I need privacy. I need to be alone while I cry because I know that I am probably going to cry.

I plop down on my unmade bed and set the envelope on my pillow. I stare at it for a few minutes and take a few deep, cleansing breaths. I'm not ready for this. I need more time, but time is running out. I glanced at my clock and see that Ethan's plane is leaving in less than three hours. If I wanted to talk to him before he gets on that plane, I need to do it sooner rather than later.

I slid my finger under the flap to break the seal. I slowly pulled out the contents and realized that this is going to be much harder than I even imagined. I'm crying even before I pick up the first item.

Open-ended. He bought me an open-ended plane ticket to London. I can go whenever I'm ready. His optimism is amazing. At least he's giving me the choice.

The next is a photo. I'm not surprised by this. There's nothing written on the back, so I can't even begin to imagine what the picture is of. I flip it over and immediately drop it to the floor. Natalie.

I remember when the picture was taken. It was our first day of senior year. Natalie, Lainey, Jill, and I were all standing in front of my car, wearing shirts that said Seniors Rule. We were all so young. We had our whole lives ahead of us still, and you could see the excitement on our faces for our last year of high school.

The letter is the last thing I look at. I know that whatever he has written is going to bring me to my knees. My love for him is so deep that I can feel my heart breaking at the thought of this being our last conversation, as one-sided as it is. His way of getting me to listen without interrupting. I have to laugh a little at that. I never have been very good at listening.

Becca,
I don't think that I have to tell you how much I love you, you should know, you should be able to feel it. I still feel it. I can feel how much you love me right now as your reading this letter and I can't even see you. As stubborn as you are at times, I might be over the Atlantic right now.

I think the contents of the envelope are self-explanatory. I still want you to be a part of my life. I want you by my side, and when the day comes that you're ready to be a part of my life again, the ticket will bring you back to me.

There's no expiration on the ticket, or my invitation. I promised you that I would love you forever and I meant it.

I gave you the picture because I wanted you to smile. I wanted you to remember a time in your life when things were less complicated. Plus, I know how much Natalie loved that photo. She always said that it was her reminder of a time when things were simpler, when life was all about what was going on next weekend instead of next month or next year. It helped her to keep life in perspective; maybe it can do the same for you.

I know that I still have a lot of explaining to do about the portrait that I sent you. The fact that you haven't mentioned it tells me that it's still wrapped. Open it, Becca. Before you read any further, open it. If you don't, then none of this will make sense.

I set the letter down and move towards my closet. I slowly opened the doors and reached in to where the package is supposed to be. It hasn't moved. It's still tucked back in the corner. The corner that I like to hide all my fears in.

I pull it out and slowly rip the packaging away, revealing not one, but two, portraits inside. They are facing each other to protect them from the elements, from damage. I can't see what they are of, but I know that

I only purchased one. He definitely has some explaining to do. I want to read ahead in his letter, find out what I'm about to see, but I don't.

I lay the two portraits face up on my floor and just stare. The portrait I purchased is on the right. I still can't believe the emotion he captured. I'm staring at it, unable to think about anything other than the fact that I ruined our relationship. My insecurities, my fears, my decisions, or lack thereof, ruined our relationship. I'm almost in a trance, staring at my own face when I glimpse at the other portrait and do a double take.

This one is also of me. My emotions are captured perfectly, of course. You can even see the tears that are running down my face. You can see the fact that I'm trying to hide my face. You can see my fear, my love, and the shock. You can see every emotion I was feeling at that moment, how uncomfortable I was, and how self-conscious I was acting. He captured me perfectly. How did I not know he was taking my picture?

I should have done my hair. I took time with it that afternoon, I remember that much, but I should have done more with it. The walking around had blown it out a little and you could see that my natural curl was fighting against the product and flat iron I had used. I still looked pretty, that much I will admit. Maybe it was the fact that all I really saw was the raw emotion that he had captured that made me like the photo so much.

I smiled but it quickly faded when I realized that he knew. He knew that I had gone to England, and that I had been to the gallery. He had seen me there and had said nothing at the time. He knew I still loved him because he knew I had come for him, and yet he had said nothing. Not a single word since then. Nothing.

The letter. He said that it would explain everything. I needed to finish that letter. I rushed back to my bed where I left it sitting. I turned to the second page and started looking for answers. I needed to know why he never said anything. Why he let me leave without him saying anything to me. He obviously knew I was there. Why had he let me walk away again?

Assuming you listened to my request (I really hope you did), you have questions. I can answer them for you, all of them, but you may not like what I have to say so you need to prepare yourself for that.

Natalie called me after you boarded the plane. She told me that you were on your way to see me. She didn't tell me why. She didn't actually tell me much of anything. She said that you were finally out of the dark hole, that you had finally let her in, and that the walls you had built around your heart were down. She asked me to be gentle with you, to "approach with caution" because she wasn't sure how you would react. I promised her I would protect your heart, always.

 I was surprised that you didn't know I was taking your picture. I couldn't help myself, I'm sorry. I knew the second you walked into the gallery, the second you arrived. My body was pulling me to you, to where you were. I had my camera on me and I took the shot. It turned out even more beautiful than I could have imagined. I went to put my camera away and that's when I knew you left. I felt your pain. I felt you run. I knew why, I knew what you saw in that picture. I saw it too. I still see it every time I look at it. The end. The end of what we had.

 I came back out hoping I was wrong, but when I didn't see you... well, my heart broke. I had lost my chance. The first chance I had truly had to win you back, to show you that I was still in love with you, and I blew it. The disappointment on my face was evident, even after I was told I had made my first sale. They didn't have to tell me which piece sold, or to whom. I already knew.

 I cancelled the purchase. Your receipt for a refund is enclosed. Think of the portraits as a gift, from me to you, of the pain that we shared and the love that we hold close to our hearts and are afraid to give to one another. I still love you, Becca. I can't say it enough. When you're ready to let me love you again, to share your love with me again, I will be here, waiting. There is no one else that I would rather spend the rest of my life with.

 You are my future, you are my everything.

Ethan

 I don't really know what to think. My heart is overwhelmed by all his beautiful words. I need to think about this. I need to figure out what I want, what my heart wants, what it can handle. The thing is, all I can think about is Ethan. He's the one I want. He's who my heart craves, who my heart belongs to. There will never be another.

 I need to get to the airport. I have less than two hours to stop him from leaving. I attempt to slide the letter back in the envelope. It's stuck on something, so I turned the envelope upside down to dump everything out. The letter floats to the bed, and the piece causing all the trouble drops on top of it.

My engagement ring. What is he trying to tell me? Does he still want to marry me? Is he proposing again? None of those explanations make sense. The only person who knows what any of this means is Ethan. I need to ask him if I want answers.

I rush down the stairs and grab my purse off the counter. I can hear Ethan speaking to me, the words from his letter fresh in my mind. I can hear Natalie pushing me. I can hear Brad's voice, telling me that he wants things to go back to the way they used to be, when we were just friends. I can hear everyone's voices, loud and clear, telling me what they want.

I stop dead in my track right outside the front door. The voices stop too. I don't need to rush to the airport. I don't need to go anywhere. He's here.

"Going somewhere?"

He's so smug sometimes. His smile tells me that he knows exactly where I was going. He knows that I was rushing to him, to find him, to stop him.

"Not anymore. I have questions and you're the only one who can answer them. I was coming to find you."

"You found me." Damn that smile! His dimple is winking at me, and my body is responding. I can see his tattoo peeking out from under his sleeve, and my body goes on high alert. I cannot allow my hormones to rule this conversation.

"I guess I did." I toss him my engagement ring. The grip I had on it has left imprints in my palm. Letting it go allowed me to realize the pain.

He caught it with ease and tosses it back to me. "That belongs to you."

"It used to. I'm not engaged anymore."

"You could be."

"No. I need to date and fall in love again before I agree to marry someone."

"I don't have much time, but would you like to go out for coffee with me? We can work on the falling in love part another time."

"I can't. See, my heart belongs to this guy I used to date. I can't really just give it away to someone else."

"He's one lucky guy then."

I smile because I miss this, our back and forth, the banter that comes so naturally. I miss talking to him without feeling like I'm about to fall apart or combust from the overwhelming emotions. I miss him. Too bad this can't last forever. I need answers.

"I still have questions, Ethan. Like, why? Why didn't you ever call, or text, or try to reach out to me?"

"Honestly?"

"Yes, please."

"I figured you wouldn't want to talk to me at first, then I figured it was too late. I was angry at myself for walking away in the beginning. Once I realized that there was no way I was going to be able to live without you, I figured it was too late. Then you came to London. I thought that maybe, if I was lucky, you came for me. That you came because you still loved me, you still wanted to be with me. When you ran, I knew I had hurt you again. I thought that maybe I was being selfish to want you in my life when all I kept doing was causing you pain. I gave up on us for a minute. Problem was, I still couldn't stop thinking about you. You were everywhere I turned. I would see you on the streets of London, or at least I thought I was seeing you. I freaked a couple people out. Then Natalie called. She told me what had happened, that she was in the hospital. She knew something bigger was wrong with her, and she was trying to push everyone away on purpose. She knew she wasn't going to make it in the end. She wanted to try and make it easier on everyone. She called me every other day until one day she didn't. I got the call from Brad instead and booked my flight while I was still on the phone with him. He told me how bad you were taking it, and I knew that you needed me. I knew that this would be my only chance to try and win you back. I knew that if you didn't still love me that I was going to have to say good-bye to you. Does that answer your question?"

He's standing so close to me. Somehow, he managed to move from the driveway to the front porch during his speech, and I didn't even notice until he stopped talking. I wanted to reach out, to touch him, but I knew if I did that, that I was a goner. There would be no turning back at that point.

"Yeah. That definitely answers my question and a bunch more that I hadn't even asked. One more thing, though. Why didn't you ever call me? You say that you thought the opportunity was gone but you never even tried. You didn't even give me the opportunity to make a decision. You made it for me."

"I don't know. I don't have a good answer for you. I wanted to call you, so many times. Honestly, I was scared. I was scared that you wouldn't want what I wanted. I was scared that you had truly moved on, and that if I called you, that I would ruin that for you. The last thing I want is to cause you more pain, Becca."

"Why now?'

"I'm tired of being scared. I'm tired of running away from everything I'm feeling. I want to be happy again, and the only way that's going to happen is if I have you back in my life. Call me selfish, but it's what I want. I wasn't sure how you would react until I saw you. The way your body responded to me, the way you leaned back into me and let me hold you. It all felt too natural. I knew you would fight it, but I knew you couldn't fight it forever. I had to make my move. I had to lay it all out on the table and take the risk. I knew you still loved me the moment I laid eyes on you before the funeral. The rest…well, the rest just happened. I let it come naturally. Everything I've done or said since that moment was because of how you reacted to me."

"I never had a choice in the matter, did I? It was never about what I wanted. My heart has been controlling my every move since the moment you walked back into my life. It wasn't a coincidence that you were at the courts the other day. What happened in the bathroom…none of this was my choice. I haven't made a single decision with my brain since you came back. Now, you're leaving, and my brain is working overtime to try and catch up with my heart. It feels like they will never be on the same page."

"I know that you're confused. I've been confused, conflicted, emotionally drained, for the last six months. I know what I want now. It took me a while to figure it out, but eventually it was clear. You. That's all I want, for the rest of my life. I want you, Becca, and I hope that you feel the same way. It may not be today or even tomorrow, but eventually one day, I hope you feel the same way. When you do, you have the ticket and the ring and you know where to find me. I'll be waiting."

I know that he means every word he said. I can feel the love radiating from his body. I wanted to respond, to tell him that today is that day, that I'm ready to spend the rest of my life with him. Of course,

Unglued

I don't. I don't say anything. He must know that I need time because he kisses me on the head and pulls me close. I hug him, I hold on for dear life, afraid that if I let go, that this will be the end of everything for us. The only thing I know right now is that I do not want this to be the end. I know I want more, I'm just not sure how much.

The second his lips touched my cheek, I felt it. Good-bye. It didn't feel final, but it was still good-bye. I knew that he was leaving our future in my hands. I knew that he was letting me make the decision. Our happiness, together or separate from each other, was in my hands. Just the thought made my heart feel heavier.

I watched him walk away. I admired the view, wondering when I would be able to pull myself together enough to be able to face him again. I knew that I wouldn't be able to stay away from him for long. I knew that my heart would cave and that I would be in London soon. I knew all of this yet I didn't say a word as he walked away. I let him walk away so that I could get my life together. I needed to be in a better place before I could be with him again.

Chapter Nineteen

I have been dreading this day all week. Normally, Friday was my favorite day of the week. Not because it was the weekend, I worked most weekends, but because it meant that I got a little "me time." I have been taking advantage of my "me time" lately. Most of it has been spent on the courts, alone. I refuse to play with anyone else right now, not that I have anyone who would dare play with me. Ethan is the only person that I can think of that would actually dare to challenge me.

Ethan. I got another text from him yesterday. It's almost like clockwork. Every Tuesday, Thursday, and Saturday at noon, I received a new text from him. They are never about anything important. It's really just him saying hello, asking me how I'm doing. It's him keeping him at the forefront of my mind. It's been almost six weeks since I've seen him, and my heart yearns for him more and more every day.

I walked into the restaurant and looked around. I finally spotted him in the far back corner with his head down. I didn't expect any less. He was still taking the loss hard. Natalie was his world, his everything. I cannot imagine what he must be feeling. I still miss her every day, so it has to be ten times worse for him.

"Hey Morgan." I try to sound upbeat, happy, but my voice cracks and betrays me. You can hear how nervous I am, how unsure I feel about seeing him. I've talked to him on the phone since the funeral, but he's been avoiding me at all costs. The only person he's seen, that I know of, is Brad. That was only once, and Brad said it was devastating to see him like that. I can see what he was talking about the second he lifts his head.

"Hey."

Not much of a talker today. There's no emotion behind his words. He's not happy to see me. He's not sad. He's empty. I can sympathize with him. I know how it feels to feel empty, like you have no one and nothing is worth living for. His heart has been ripped out. I wonder if this is how I was after Ethan left.

I slide into the booth seat across from him, but I have no idea what to say. Nothing is going to take his pain away. Nothing is going to lessen everything he feels right now. They say that time heals all wounds. I believe that's true, but how much time is enough time to heal Morgan? I know that I will never be the same without Natalie in my life. I know that Morgan will never be the same either, and I'm scared for him. I'm scared that he will never come close to being the amazing person that he once was. I don't want to see this destroy him.

The waitress comes over and I order a cup of coffee, Morgan orders water. She walks away and returns moments later with our drinks. I let her know that I will flag her down when we're ready to order. I'm pretty sure this upsets her since she walks away without acknowledging what I just said. There goes her tip.

I'm still at a loss for words. I want to ask him how he's doing. It's the most natural way to start a conversation. The sad part is that I know how he's doing, and he's not doing that great. I need a mutual subject. Natalie. *Crap!* She's always been our common ground. She was the link in our friendship.

I need for you to take care of him, to help him through this, to make sure that he moves on. I want him to lead a full life. I want him to find someone to spend his life with, to marry, to have children and grow old with.

I can hear Natalie's voice. I want to scream. How? How am I supposed to do that? I can barely figure out how to have a conversation with him. How was I supposed to help him move on? I have barely moved on.

"So...um, have you registered for classes yet?"

School. That was the best thing I could come up with to break the ice. He's staring at me like a deer caught in the headlights. I see his mouth start to curve up in the right corner, and I must have looked confused because he starts to laugh at me. Not a little chuckle, either. I can feel people turning to stare at Morgan because he's laughing so hard and incredibly loud.

"What?"

"I'm sorry. It's just…I know why you're here. School, really? That's the best ice breaker you can come up with. I'm devastated over here. I've just lost my best friend, the love of my life, and you want to talk about school?"

It took me a minute to realize that while he was talking, he also started to cry. Talking about Natalie, even though he hadn't said her name, had brought him to tears. I don't know what else to do, so I trust my guts for once and reach over to take his hand.

"I'm sorry. I'm obviously not very good at this. This was the stuff that Natalie used to take care of for us. This is the crap that she loved to do. She loved helping us pick up the pieces of our lives and glue them back together. She loved taking care of us, all of us."

This brought a small smile to his face. It wasn't a sad smile, either. It was genuine, like he was glad that I had noticed that about her, remembered that about her.

"She sure did. I thought she was never going to come down from the high she got after Ethan left you."

Ouch! That kind of stung but I'll take it. He's talking. He's talking and it's about Natalie. From what I understand, I've accomplished more in the last five minutes than anyone else has in the last six weeks.

"Yeah, well, I wouldn't have wanted her to float away so I had to pull myself out of it. She helped of course. I couldn't have done it without her. I couldn't have done it without either of you."

"You know, she always thought that you and Ethan would get back together, we all did. I know you two had a few run-ins while he was here. What happened?"

"That's what you want to talk about? Me and Ethan?"

"I don't really want to talk about anything. What I want most right now is the remote control, and our, my bed."

"See, its things like that. You said 'our' but you caught yourself. It's okay to still say those things. It's okay to miss her. It's okay to wish she was here, to mourn your loss, to feel sad every day. I don't want you to think that I'm worried about you because you're sad. We're all worried about you because it feels like a large part of you died when Natalie did."

"But I did. She was my life. When she died, I did to."

"I should make you read the letter she wrote me. She loved you so much, you know that. Not just because she was going to marry you. Not the kind of love that most people experience in a lifetime. She loved you more than she loved herself. She wants more for you than what you have right now. I don't think it's much of a stretch that she *expects* more from you than what you are right now."

"It's funny how well you knew her. Lainey called last week, and some of the things she said just didn't make any sense. It's like she had no idea who Natalie even was. Jill too. You only knew her for the last five years; they grew up together."

"It's not how long I knew her that matters, it's how well I understood her. She was a complex person. There were more sides to that girl than I can even begin to describe. You know all of them as well as I do, maybe even better."

"Yeah, I guess you're right. She was amazing, though. The only person I have ever known that could juggle as much as she was and still somehow come out on top."

"What do you mean?"

"Well, she was planning the wedding, bringing you back from your own personal hell, taking a full load of classes, working almost full time, and putting up with me on a daily basis. After all of that was said and done, she still found time to clean the house, go to the movies with me, laugh with her friends over coffee, and spend time alone with her favorite book. She was amazing."

"Yeah, she was." Do I tell him the reason I'm here? Do I tell him what Natalie wrote about him in my letter? I think it will help. I think he needs to hear it. "You know, she's still bossing us all around without even being here. Just yesterday, she whispered in my ear to stop drinking so much coffee. I decided against another cup, and two seconds later, I was nauseated. It's almost like she knew it wasn't going to agree with me. I hear her voice all the time, telling me what to do."

He was quiet for a minute, like he was deciding if he should tell me what was on his mind or not. The look on his face had me puzzled. He wasn't upset, but he wasn't happy. His mood had changed to something in-between. It almost looked like acceptance.

"I talked to her yesterday. I know it sounds crazy, believe me, I know, but I really did. I fell asleep on the couch and there she was. It was so real, Becca. I was so caught off guard that I didn't say anything at first, I just stared at her. Finally, she sat down next to me, and I had an entire conversation with her."

I knew what he was talking about. I could tell that the thought of it alone was overwhelming him. I remember the first time that I saw Natalie, when I was in her bathroom, before Ethan and Brad cornered me. It was overwhelming. Hearing about his experience was just as overwhelming, for me and for him.

"I believe you. What did she say?"

"Not much. She said that she loved me too much to watch me fall apart and that if I didn't get my act together that she wouldn't come back and see me again. I can still hear her voice."

"I hear it all the time. I see her sometimes too, so I know how crazy it sounds. I've never told anyone but it feels good to get it off my chest. She's trying to tell us something, I think."

"In the letter she wrote me, she told me that this would happen. That I would be like this, depressed and unwilling to pull myself out of it. She told me that one day, you and I would have a conversation and that I was supposed to listen to everything you said and move on with my life. She told me this would happen."

"She made this happen. She made me promise to take care of you. She made me promise to help you move on with your life, to find someone new to spend it with. I know that sounds painful right now. I know you don't have any plans to do that any time soon. Just know that I'm here to always help you remember her, even once you have moved on. She wouldn't want us to forget her but to carry her in our hearts, forever."

That was it. I had said what I needed to say. Done what was asked of me. I felt better about keeping my promise to Natalie, even though she never gave me much of a choice. I knew that she would have done the same for me if the situation had been reversed.

Don't waste any more time not being together. Life is way too short for that.

An hour later, we both got up from the table with a smile on our face. Morgan was starting to sound like the person I've always known, and my head and my heart were a little lighter. I knew that Morgan was going to be okay. Not tomorrow or the next day, but someday soon. He will always keep Natalie in his heart—we all will—but he was going to make room for someone else someday because that's what Natalie would have wanted him to do.

As for me, I learned a great deal about myself after talking with Morgan. Everything that he was going through right now, I had already been there. It was interesting, seeing what I had gone through from the other side. I realized that I would not have made it if I had not been blessed with such amazing friends. Natalie, Morgan, and Brad had pulled me back, and I was now determined to help pull Morgan back.

I went to throw some money down on the table to cover my coffee when I realized that I never even touched it. I sat through an entire conversation and never even took a sip. On any other day, during any other conversation, I would have at least drank half a pot, and the waitress would have been excited when I left. I guess things really are changing.

∞

With school about to be over for the summer, I found that my mind was more occupied. It was nice to have a break from thinking about Natalie all the time, or Ethan, or Brad. Speaking of Brad, he and I have finally found our comfort zone again. It took a while, but we have successfully managed to get back to where we used to be.

We found out pretty quickly that we needed to set some ground rules to our friendship. Rule number one…no more kissing! Rule number two…no more sleepovers. We may never have consummated our relationship, but it was still weird to have him in my bed knowing that I was once again thinking about Ethan.

Ethan. His texts are like clockwork. No matter where I am or what I'm doing, I always have my phone by my side when I know that it's time for him to text me. We're rebuilding our relationship. We didn't have to start from scratch like I thought we would, but we started as close to the beginning as possible. We had both grown during our time apart and we were different, as slight as it was. We needed to get to know the people we had become, the person that had emerged on the other side of the tragedy.

It's approaching seven o'clock in London right now, the normal time for him to text me. I hear the tower clock at the center of campus chime for the noon hour, and at the same time, my phone vibrates in my pocket. I don't even have to look to know that it's him.

Ethan: Just wanted to say hello, let you know that I was thinking about you today, like every other day. Talked to Morgan yesterday and he sounds better, at least I think he sounds better. I love you, Becca, forever."

He's always signs off the same way since we've started to communicate again. I couldn't help but smile knowing that he loved me, that there was still hope for us yet.

I walked into class, my last one of the summer, ready to take my exam, and have a few weeks off before getting back to the grind. I've made a ton of progress in the last three months. I will be on schedule to graduate in the spring like I had originally planned. I thought that maybe taking the spring semester off would set me back, but it didn't.

My phone alerts me to a new text. I take a look to see that Brad is waiting for me at my house, packed and ready to leave for our road trip. Morgan was coming along, too. We all decided that we needed to get out of the city for a while, take a break from our new reality and relax. Morgan was less than enthusiastic but he realized, pretty quickly, that I wasn't going to give up on him coming with us.

Las Vegas was our destination of choice. Not exactly a relaxing atmosphere but a place where all your problems can disappear, at least for a while. Plus, I was in the mood to play some slots. I didn't have a lot of money to gamble but the little that I had saved, I was probably going to be donating to a slot machine in my near future.

I breezed through my last final and rushed home. The boys will be waiting on me. I have yet to pack and I have no idea what I wanted to bring. The nightlife there is incredible from what I've heard, and we'll be seeing the sights during the daytime. This means that I need to bring almost my entire closet, less the winter clothing.

I greeted each of them with a passing hello and bounded up the stairs as quickly as possible. I want to get on the road so that we can make it there before dark. It's only a seven-hour drive but it's going to be a very long seven hours in the car with two men.

Unglued

I shoved a variety of clothes in my suitcase, not bothering to fold anything neatly. This would have bothered Natalie to no end. Sometimes I think I do things like that, the little things, just to see if she will appear and curse me out. It has yet to work. I have not caught sight of her or heard her voice in a while, and I'm starting to miss it.

I headed into the bathroom and gathered up my personal items. Reaching under the sink, I grabbed for my travel bag and knocked over the open box of tampons. An alarm goes off in my head, realizing that I haven't needed to use them in a long time. I counted backwards, quickly trying to figure out the last time I had my period, and I can't seem to remember. It's been over a month, that's all I know.

Crap!

It must be from the stress. I missed my period a couple of times after I hurt myself. The doctor told me that when I stress myself out that my body can react to that and change. I don't know how accurate that information is, but right now, it's all I have to go on. I have to push the thought aside so that we can get going.

I'm just finishing shoving my makeup in the side pocket of my duffel when Brad walks through my bedroom door. He glances around at the luggage that's accumulated and shakes his head. Without saying a word, he grabs both suitcases and heads back downstairs. I followed behind him with my purse and my duffel bag.

The drive to Vegas goes quicker than I thought it would. We made it in just over six and a half hours. Brad's foot was heavy on the gas pedal the entire way. As the city comes into view, I see nothing but lights, lots of them. It's just past nine o'clock, and even though the sun has yet to disappear on the horizon, it's just dark enough to make the city look incredible.

We checked in, headed to our room and dropped our luggage. I can tell that the boys just got a burst of energy, so did I. It's nice to see Morgan smile, Brad too. Both of them have been so serious lately, bordering on depressed and not much fun to be around. When Brad suggested a road trip, I knew that I had to come to make sure that they stayed out of trouble. Plus, I can hear the slots screaming my name from our room.

We were sharing a room to save money. It had two beds, and tonight will be the first time in over a month that Brad and I have shared a sleeping space. I have been mentally preparing myself. I figured as long as I had a few cocktails, it wouldn't matter when I passed out.

We headed back down to the casino floor and stood in awe of what was going on around us. The sounds, the lights, the people. There was so much going on. It was almost like I was going to burst from excitement.

"I'm going to find a slot machine and blow some money. Where are you boys headed?"

They gave each other a mischievous look and both said "out" at the same time.

"Okay. Should we meet back here at a certain time or am I going to be fast asleep before you boys come back?"

"We'll be back before dawn." The look I gave him must have made him think twice about his answer. "I'm kidding. We should be back in a few hours."

"Where exactly are you going?"

"Um, well…it's guy's night. Can we leave it at that?"

Brad's answer was evasive. He didn't want to tell me where they were headed, and it was starting to sound like I didn't want to know what they were up to. Morgan was smiling, Brad was smiling, and in the end, that was all that really mattered to me.

"Fine. I'll be down here for a while, but I'm kind of tired, so try and be quiet when you come back. If you need me just give me a call. I've got my phone on me."

"Sounds like a plan. Ready, Brad?"

Morgan was finally starting to act like the person that I had grown to love over the years. He was upbeat and most importantly, living his life again.

They took off in one direction and I headed to a bank of slot machines that looked like fun. I knew that I was going to lose. We were staying for three days, and I had to make my money last. I put a twenty in the machine and placed my bet. I hit some kind of crazy bonus game on my first spin and before I knew it, I was up a hundred dollars and two hours had flown by.

My excitement was dulled by the fact that my body was drained of all its energy. I cashed out my ticket at the closest machine and headed straight for the elevators. I was going to try and get some sleep before the guys got back. I had a feeling that they were out drinking and drunk boys don't know how to be quiet.

I showered and changed. The second my head hit the pillow, I was struggling to keep my eyes open. I found an old movie that was about to start but was asleep before they even rolled the opening credits.

"*You know, you really should be taking better care of yourself. I warned you about how much coffee you were drinking, didn't I?*"
"*What are you talking about? I gave up coffee completely. It lost its appeal a while ago.*"
"*Did you ever wonder why?*"
"*Maybe because I spend all day serving coffee to other people. Honestly, now that I don't drink it, I can barely stand the smell of it.*"
"*Funny. You gave it up and can't stand the smell of it. Give anything else up lately?*"
What was she getting at? I still love coffee I just don't drink it any more. The smell is nauseating. She did this to me. My subconscious must be working for her these days.
"*No. Other than coffee, I am the same person that you've always known.*"
"*Fine. So, how's tennis going?*"
"*Stupid question but how did you know I was playing again. I didn't start until after...*"
"*After I died. It's okay to say it you know. It's not like I can get mad about it or change the situation. I'm dead, you're alive, case closed. So, tennis?*"
"*It's fine but it wears me out. I can only play for so long before my shoulder is screaming at me to stop and most days, I'm so tired that I stop before I even get to that point.*"
"*So, you're always tired, you can't stand certain smells...anything else weird going on right now?*"
"*What's this about, Natalie? Not that I'm complaining but I haven't seen you in weeks and now here you are, being all weird about stuff. What's going on?*"
"*I can't tell you, you have to figure it out for yourself.*"
"*Well, let's talk about something else then because this conversation is irritating the crap out of me.*"
"*Okay, what would you like to talk about? How's Ethan?*"
"*He's fine, so is everyone else.*" *I wonder how much she really knows, how much she sees. Am I really even seeing her?* "*You know, Morgan is here with us.*"

"I know. I talked to him last night. He's doing better. He seems like he's at least trying to be happy."

"He is. I know that this is hard on him; his wound is still fresh even though it's been over a month. I think once school starts back up that he'll start to move on."

"I'm glad. It's been hard watching him the last few weeks. In the beginning it wasn't easy watching him mourn, but I think the fact that he's mourning less is actually harder for me to watch. I don't want him to forget about me."

"I don't think that's possible."

"So, seven weeks, huh? It's been that long already? Wow! Time really flies right by doesn't it?"

"I guess it does."

"Just keep something in mind for me, Becca. If you're not choosing to live life to the fullest each and every day, then you're allowing yourself to die, one missed moment at a time. I don't want that for you, for any of you. I want you all to live your lives to the fullest."

What do you say to your best friend who is watching everything but experiencing nothing? She can see it all as it unfolds, knows more than we do, but yet can't help us or talk to us or stop us from making mistakes. She's helpless and it must be driving her nuts after being a meddler for so long.

"Well, I better get going. Morgan's waiting for me. I promised him that I would pop in and see him again tonight if he didn't get too drunk."

"Natalie, before you go can I ask you something?"

"Sure, what's up?"

"Are you doing okay? I know it sounds stupid but we all have each other and we are trying our best to move on without you here, carrying you in our hearts, but you are all alone."

"I'm okay. I get to watch the people I love live their lives, and that's enough for me right now. One day I'll stop visiting you, and you'll know that I've made my peace, that I've decided to move on."

"Not that I don't love talking to you and miss you every day but I hope you find peace, Natalie. I really do."

I awoke with a start. I always freak out after talking to Natalie. It seemed so real, like if I tried, I could reach out and touch her, hug her, pull her back into my reality. I know that's not possible. I know that she's gone. That doesn't mean that I don't wish things had turned out differently.

My stomach started to turn. I smelled cigarette smoke and beer and it's overwhelming my senses. The guys are sound asleep. Brad is snoring softly next to me. It's rising higher. I can feel it in my throat.

I dart to the bathroom and make it to the toilet just in time. I puked up the entire contents of my stomach, and when I am finally done dry-heaving, I lay down on the tile floor. It's cooling on my skin. I don't feel sick. I don't have a fever. Now that I've puked, I feel much better, actually.

I stood up and splashed some water on my face. I can taste vomit. I reach for my toothbrush and put a dab of toothpaste on it as Brad walks in the bathroom. I can hear him peeing. The smell of beer and cigarette smoke fills the room, and my stomach turns again. I puked right in the sink.

Without saying a word, Brad leaves the bathroom, and I puked again as he passes me. Either he is sleepwalking, or he's so drunk that he didn't even realized I was standing there. Either is an option with as strong as the scent of beer is.

I rinsed the sink, brushed my teeth, and head back into the room. I can see that the sun is peeking over the horizon, so I open the curtains. The smells are lingering in the room, so I decided to dress and head down to get some breakfast. My stomach is empty and if I stay any longer I will probably puke again.

Chapter Twenty

Our hotel has three restaurants and a buffet. I opted for the buffet not knowing what I really wanted to try and eat after puking so much this morning. It has a variety of fresh fruit, yogurt, and an omelet bar. My stomach growled as I passed the buffet and followed the host to my table. She drops three menus on the table and heads back to her stand without saying anything.

I send a quick text to both of the guys, letting them know that I am down at the buffet getting breakfast. I get a response from Morgan that he's on his way. Brad never responds. He must still be passed out.

"Good morning, sunshine. What time did you boys get in last night?"

"More like this morning. I had to drag Brad back here, literally. He was trying to go home with a stripper."

"So that's where you guys went last night."

"Don't tell him I told you. I don't think he wanted you to know."

"I won't but just for the record, I don't really care where you guys went as long as you had fun."

"It was okay. Not really my scene if you know what I mean."

I knew what he was referring to. I could tell that Morgan had rolled out of bed and come right down at the mention of breakfast. His hair was tussled, and his shirt was wrinkled from sleeping, but I couldn't detect the smell of beer oozing from him like I did with Brad this morning.

"So, you hungry?"

"Yes, I'm famished. I puked twice this morning and now I'm running on empty."

"You threw up? Are you feeling okay?"

I have to really think about it for a minute as I stared down at my plate. It's overflowing with food. I have toast stacked on top of eggs and bacon and sausage. I put my fruit on top of my yogurt, and I have hash browns in my hand with no place to put them.

"Yeah. I feel all right, just hungry now I guess."

Morgan is also staring at my plate with wide eyes. I put the hash browns back, knowing that I could always return if I really wanted them. That's why it's a buffet. I don't have to cram everything on my plate at once. Plus, they make these plates so small. They want you to make more than one trip.

I dropped my plate off at the table and headed in the direction of the beverage station. I see Brad approaching, looking like he needs a shower, a shave, and about five more hours of sleep. He's still a few feet away when I catch a whiff of him. The smell immediately makes me nauseous and I run to the nearest trashcan.

I feel bad for the people around me, watching, but I can't help it. Brad comes up behind me and I puke again. Between sobs, because now I'm crying from embarrassment. I tell him to go away and to have Morgan bring me a glass of water.

"So, seven weeks, huh? It's been that long already?"

"So, you're always tired, you can't stand certain smells..."

Oh! My! God!

There was no way I could be pregnant. I haven't had sex with anyone since...*Crap!* Ethan. I forgot about the bathroom. Still, I've had my period...*Crap!* I still haven't figured that out. When was the last time? Natalie and I were on the same cycle.

Crap! Crap! Crap!

I take the glass of water Morgan hands me and down it. My hands are shaking and I feel like I might faint. I need something to sit on. Morgan must have read my mind because he's pulling a chair over for me and helping me into it. I can see Brad standing by our table. He looks hurt and confused.

"Tell him I'm sorry for yelling at him but he smells awful."

"So, you want me to apologize to him for you and then tell him he smells awful?"

"Yes. Tell him that he needs to go shower and wash the stripper off of him before his scent makes me puke again." I'm dead serious but Morgan is looking at me like I'm crazy. "Seriously. Go tell him because I don't have anything left in my stomach, and he's standing between me and my food. I want to go eat."

"Okay. I'll get rid of him."

I watch as Morgan tells Brad what I told him to. Now he looks really hurt. As soon as he's gone, I make my way over to the table and pull my plate in front of me. I dig in, the smell of the food a welcome scent compared to Brad. My stomach thanks me by growling loudly, twice, as I down my entire plate in a matter of minutes. Morgan is just sitting there, watching me, with his mouth hanging open.

"Close your mouth. I told you I was hungry."

"I know but…you just ate enough for two people, and it looks like you could go back for more."

Two people. *Crap!* I'm gonna puke again.

I dash back to the trashcan and up comes everything I just consumed. It does not taste as good the second time.

Morgan brings me another glass of water, and I drink it slowly this time. Maybe I do have a virus. Maybe I am getting sick. Maybe it's something other than the one thing that I know it probably is.

"You want to go lay down or something? Do you think you can make it back upstairs without puking?"

"Yeah. I can make it, but you can stay here. Eat and pack me up some food for later. I'm going to be hungry again once I stop puking."

I slept until close to dinnertime. When I finally woke up, I found a note from the boys that they are playing blackjack and to come and find them so we can go to dinner.

P.S. I made Brad shower again while you were sleeping.

That brings a smile to my face. I felt bad for blaming it on Brad, but I knew that it was his smell, the smell of beer and cigarettes, that was making me sick to my stomach. If I could avoid those two smells until we get back home, I would be fine. Problem with that was that almost everyone in Vegas was either smoking or drinking or both. In Vegas, everyone is allowed to walk down the sidewalk with a drink in their hands. Tonight was going to be challenging.

I made it through the next couple of days without another puking incident. Maybe I really was just catching a bug. I would believe that if I wasn't sleeping all the time. I fell asleep by the pool after sleeping for over ten hours the night before. I slept the entire trip home and went straight to bed as soon as Brad dropped me off.

Now to find out what is really going on with me? All the boxes look the same. They all promise accuracy and quick results. Some have lines, others have plus or minus signs and then some even say "pregnant" or "not pregnant."

Crap!

These are the times when Natalie would be the person I would call. She would tell me to close my eyes and pick a box; that I was going to get the same results no matter what. She would be right. I was over-thinking it, and no matter which brand I chose, it was going to tell me that I was pregnant. Maybe I should save myself the embarrassing purchase and just go to the doctor and pee on a stick there?

No. I can do this. I can buy this nice blue and white box in front of me, and let it tell me that I'm pregnant. No counting lines, no decoding plus or minus signs. I was going to buy the one that spelled it out for me.

Aside from the lady who cashed me out giving me a funny look, the trip was less embarrassing than I thought it was going to be. I tossed my purchase in my passenger's seat and headed home. My mom should be fast asleep and my sister wasn't coming home from her trip to Italy until tomorrow, so I shouldn't have to worry about anyone seeing me. Still, I slip it into my purse just in case.

The results are what I expect them to be. I'm pregnant. The box says that the test is supposed to take up to five minutes before it gives you your results. Mine was done in less than two. I was either super pregnant or farther along than most people when they take these tests.

I pick up the evidence and put it back in the bag from the drugstore. I don't want to tell my mom yet. I know she will be supportive. I'm not scared to tell her. I'm scared that once I tell someone else that it becomes real. I'm single, living at home with my mom, still in college, and now pregnant.

What about Ethan? How do I tell him? I was just starting to feel like we were on track and that I was ready to see if maybe we still had a future together. Well, I know the answer to that question. Ready or not we have a future together, at least for the next eighteen years or so. I need to call him, tell him. If I'm as far along as I think I am, as far along as I know I have to be, then I will probably start showing sooner rather than later. I don't want someone else to tell him.

I'm depositing the evidence in the trash can outside when Brad pulls up. For some reason I want to tell him. I want to run to him and tell him. I don't, knowing that the reality of the situation is that I need to keep it a secret, at least until I find a way to tell Ethan.

"Hey. What's going on?"

"Not much. What are you doing here?"

"I can't seem to find my MP3 player, and I was hoping that it ended up in your bag. I checked everywhere else so you're my last hope. If you don't have it then I probably left it in the hotel room."

"Oh. I haven't unpacked yet. You're welcome to look through my bags if you want. I left them all sitting in the living room."

We headed inside and together took my bags up to my room. I was trying to act casual. I can feel that I'm close to the edge. I wanted to burst with excitement. My situation is not even close to ideal, but I can't help but feel excited. Having a baby is a blessing. My blessing is coming at a very inconvenient time, but I don't care.

We found Brad's MP3 player and he took off. I did the math and realized that it's past midnight now in England. I should have sent Ethan a text. I should have called him as soon as I found out. Maybe I got a false positive. Those tests can't always be accurate. Maybe I should make an appointment with the doctor just to make sure.

The doctor confirms what the test said—I'm pregnant. We did the math since I know when the baby was conceived, and he estimated that I am due in early April. I have four days before school starts back up. That gives me this weekend to find a way to tell Ethan.

I left the doctor's office and headed for work. I'm running late, and there's so much on my mind that I don't even see the other car coming. I remember a flash of light, the sound of the cars hitting, and the pain in my shoulder. After that, everything goes black.

When I wake up, I'm in the hospital. I immediately know why, and my hand goes to my stomach. I have a brace on my right shoulder, but it doesn't appear that anything else is wrong with me. I'm not attached to any machines. I don't even have an IV in my arm.

Unglued

The sound of a crash down the hall flashes me back to the accident. I hear the metal scrapings, the loud boom, but I also hear something else, something quieter. I glance over at the clock on the wall and see that it's after three. My appointment was at eleven, and it took about forty minutes. It must have been close to noon when the accident happened.

Ethan. That sound was my phone.

I scoot to the side of the bed and stand. I need to call my mom. I need to find out about my car. I need to get home and pack.

I can't sit around, I don't have time. I remember what I was thinking about. I was thinking about going to London. I was thinking about going to Ethan, telling him about the baby, telling him I was ready.

A nurse comes around the corner and greets me with a warm smile.

"I see you are awake and moving around okay."

"Yes. I'm fine. Can I go home now?"

"I understand that being here is not fun, but the doctor has been waiting for you to wake up so he can examine you. I will page him, and then, he will let you know when you can go home. Your mom is on her way here right now."

"Thanks. Do you know how long before the doctor comes in?"

"Let me go page him. It shouldn't be too long."

She leaves and my mom appears moments later, tears in her eyes. She almost knocks me over as she wraps her arms around me.

"Mom, I'm fine. Look, all in one piece."

"You scared me. They said you were in an accident but that you were fine. Your car is totaled. I guess they had to cut you out."

"I'm not worried about my car. I just want to get out of here."

Like magic, the doctor appears.

"So, you want to go home? You're gonna have to let me check you out first. Okay?"

"Yeah, that's fine. Anything to get me out of here faster."

"All right, hop back up on the bed then so I can check you out."

He does a quick once over and then picks up my chart and studies it for a minute. He comes back over and starts to examine my stomach, and I realized what he saw on my chart. Before I can stop him, he outs me to my mom.

"Well, it doesn't appear that the baby was injured in the accident. All of your tests came back fine, and your abdomen isn't swollen. I would say that you both were pretty lucky. I will get your paperwork drawn up so you can get out of here. You need to make sure you take it easy for the next few days, and if you have any spotting or pains, you need to come back and see us right away, okay?"

Crap!

I nod because the way my mom is looking at me right now has caused my throat to tighten and my airway to close. I can barely breathe, let alone speak.

The doctor leaves and my mom takes a seat on the bed next to me. I should have just told her when I first found out. Now, I was going to have to deal with the repercussions of hiding it from her.

"So, I'm going to be a grandma?"

"Yeah."

"Were you planning on telling me anytime soon?"

"Um, yeah."

"Are you planning on telling Brad?"

"Yeah."

"Well, since you weren't shocked by what the doctor said like I was, I'm assuming you've gone to the doctor already."

"Yeah."

"When are you due?"

"April."

"Okay. We'll start cleaning out the guest room in the next few weeks and turn that into the nursery. The baby can sleep in your room with you and Brad until…"

"What?"

"That's how it's done, honey. The baby sleeps in your room until its old enough to sleep through the night."

"Okay. I get that part, or at least I will, but what does that have to do with Brad?" Realization dawned on me a little too late. She thought that Brad was the father. Why wouldn't she? We were still dating when I got pregnant. "Wait. Mom, Brad's not the father. Not that you need to know this, but Brad and I never slept together, not like that."

"Okay. Well then, who is, Becca? I really hope you weren't out sleeping around on Brad because if I do the math right you got pregnant right about the time Natalie died. I know that you were an emotional wreck but that's no excuse."

"Thanks for the vote of confidence, Mom, but I wasn't sleeping around. I've only slept with one person."

Unglued

I could see it in her eyes when she realized that I meant Ethan. I saw the moment she realized that Ethan was the father. I saw the moment it all connected, and then I saw her smile. True happiness beamed from her smile.

"Well then, okay. I think you might have a flight to catch."

"I couldn't agree with you more. Let's get me out of here."

Epilogue

The day I showed up at the gallery in London was the best day of my life. I walked in and was immediately surrounded by photos of myself again. This time, I wasn't embarrassed or ashamed. I wasn't self-conscious at all. I was beaming with happiness as I walked from portrait to portrait, waiting for Ethan to realize I was there.

I felt him. I knew he was close and getting closer. I was nervous to see him, to tell him the news. The only people I had told so far were my mom, who the doctor told by accident, and Natalie. Before leaving for London I made my mom take me to the cemetery.

Sitting in front of a stone talking to her was surreal. It made it a little too real that she was actually gone. I hadn't been to the cemetery, hadn't seen her beautiful headstone. I had avoided it at all costs so far, but somehow it felt right.

> *Loving daughter, wife and friend. May you live on in our hearts forever.*

That's how Natalie would have wanted to be remembered. I was surprised when I saw that it said wife instead of fiancée. Natalie had been calling herself Morgan's wife for a long time, even before he had proposed to her. She would have wanted to be remembered that way. In all aspects of their life they were married, except for the piece of paper. That piece of paper doesn't change the fact that they loved each other and will always love each other.

I haven't spoken to Natalie since Vegas. It's been less than a week but it feels like it's been forever. I really wanted to tell her in person, or rather, in my dreams. Somehow, it would have made it more real. Somehow, I think she already knew.

He's really close now. The hair on the back of my neck is tingling and I have goose bumps forming on my arms and legs.

I feel a familiar set of arms slide around my waist. I resist the urge to jump. I know that he won't notice the two pounds I've gained, but I know they are there.

"It's about time. My heart started pounding hours ago. I knew you were here."

"Really? Hours ago? What time?"

"I don't know. About ten this morning, I guess. What time did you get in? You must have taken an overnight flight."

How does he know these things? I landed just after ten this morning. I took a red-eye flight that left Tucson at seven last night. He wasn't supposed to know I was coming. I wonder if my mom called him.

"So, are you psychic now? You forgot to tell me about your abilities." I turn to face him sporting a crooked grin to make sure he knew I was picking on him and not serious. "What am I thinking about right now?"

He leaned in really close and whispered in my ear. I couldn't contain my laugh. His thoughts were naughty and not even close to what I was thinking.

"Not even close."

"Well, that's what I was thinking about the moment I laid eyes on you."

"Will you settle for a kiss?" I pouted at him, like I would be disappointed if he didn't accept.

"I wouldn't exactly call that settling."

His lips met mine and the world around me exploded. Nothing would ever compare to the way kissing Ethan made me feel. It was like fireworks were going off inside of me. His naughty thoughts were starting to become rather appealing.

"Well, hello to you to." It was all I could manage once he finally broke our connection. There were at least half a dozen pairs of eyes on us, but I didn't care. The only thing I cared about at that moment was the fact that I was standing face to face with Ethan, and I was about to tell him our big news.

"That's not how I say hello, but it will have to do for now." His dimple is winking at me. I'm a goner. I've been around him for less than five minutes and I already want to lose all my clothes.

"We'll have to work on that."

"So, did you fly all this way to kiss me or is there something else you want to tell me?"

Crap!

"I did not fly all this way just to kiss you. I thought that maybe it was time."

"Time for what? What are you saying?"

I can hear the excitement in his voice, it's unmistakable. He's not even trying to hide it. The smile that's plastered across his face is not helping his cause any either.

"It's time to move on...together."

He picks me up and spins me around before I even realize what's going on. The movement is causing my stomach to turn. I cannot puke right now. That would not be good. That would be really bad actually. I haven't told him yet. I want to make sure that he wants me first. I need him to want to be with me because he loves me, not because I'm pregnant.

He sets me back down and I close my eyes to calm my stomach. It's working. It's working. It's not working. I open my eyes and dart through the closest door and into what looks like an office. I find the trashcan and empty my stomach.

Ethan's standing behind me when I turn to leave. He looks confused, but his excitement to see me is hiding just beneath the surface.

"You okay?"

"Yeah. I just got a little dizzy and all that spinning went to my head, and my stomach I guess."

"Are you sure? You look like you need to sit down for a minute and rest."

"I do, but I'm fine, really."

He brings two chairs over to where I am, and we sit in silence for a few minutes. I know he has questions. I know he needs answers that only I can give him.

"So, do you still want me? Even after watching me puke?"

"I would have held your hair back if I had made it in here fast enough."

"I take that as a yes."

"Yes. Absolutely. Definitely."

"Good. I want to be with you too. I want to spend the rest of my life with you. But there is something I need to ask you."

"Okay."

"At the end of the day, after everything is said and done, after we lay it all out on the table, I need to know that you will love me no matter what, that I'm yours, and that your feelings for me will never change."

"No matter what happens, no matter what you say or do, I plan on loving you until the day I die. I will never let you go again. You belong to me and only me, and that's the way it's supposed to be. We were meant to be together, Becca. It's always been me and you, and it always will be."

I need to tell him. I need to do it now before I chicken out, and he asks me why I'm fat in a few months. That would be bad. Wake up one morning and say "oh, by the way honey, I'm five months pregnant."

"No, it won't be. It's always been you and me, you're right, but it won't always be that way. It's not that way right now."

"What are you saying, Becca? Is there someone else that I need to know about?"

"Yes and no. There is someone else, but it's not what you're thinking."

"Then what is it? Because all I can see right now is red and Brad's face. I don't want to go down this path again."

"You don't have to." I can see how upset he is. I need to just tell him. All this beating around the bush is causing problems already. I promised to always be honest with him a long time ago. It's now or never. "It's not going to be just us this time around. I'm pregnant. We're pregnant."

I never thought that I could say anything to bring Ethan to his knees. I saw his eyes get wide, then glaze over, then roll back in his head. He hit the floor with a loud thump and was out cold. I knew that he wouldn't be out for long. He was going to come to and have questions.

He came to after about only five minutes. He was groggy, and I helped him back into his chair. He was looking between my face and my belly. I'm not sure if he was looking for confirmation, but he wasn't going to find it there. I wasn't showing yet and the doctor said that I probably wouldn't start to show for at least another month or so.

I gave him a few minutes to let it sink in. It took me a day to really believe that I was pregnant. He wasn't going to get that much time.

"So..."

"I don't know what to say, Becca. That's the last thing that I thought I was going to hear today. I'm going to be a dad."

"You are going to be a dad."

"Are you sure. I mean, not that it's mine, but are you sure you are pregnant."

"I took a home test and went to the doctor. Then I got in a car accident and the hospital told me I was pregnant."

"Are you okay? Is the baby okay?"

"We're fine. I was pretty lucky. Somehow my stomach didn't have a single mark on it from the accident. It's almost like something was protecting my stomach."

"So, we're having a baby?"

"Yeah. We're having a baby."

I wanted to ask if he still wanted to be with me. This changed everything. Our relationship would change. It wasn't just about us, about what we wanted anymore. It was about our child, what they needed. Our world was about to change.

∞

I'm finally starting to show. Yesterday was the first time I wore maternity pants. I've been avoiding the fact that my pants were getting tighter and tighter. When my button popped off as I sat down to breakfast, I knew I had no choice, but to acknowledge the fact that I had put on baby weight.

I cried, of course. I cry about a lot of things these days, most things. My emotions run the spectrum, from one end to the other, on a daily basis. I never know what will set me off or make me cry. It's a battle, but when I'm happy, I'm super happy.

I'm not sure why I ever questioned his love for me. The last two months have been the best of my life. They have not been easy, but they have been the best. He's been by my side every step of the way, riding the rollercoaster of emotions every day, and taking everything in stride.

He's going to be home in about five minutes, and I'm trying to make tonight special. We moved in together when he came back from London last month. It's been different, challenging at times. I think a lot of it has to do with my emotional rollercoaster. Some of it has to do with the fact that neither of us are the same people we used to be.

The little things are the same, and the important things are the same. It's all the stuff in-between that we fight about. He prefers a different kind of milk now. I want us both to eat healthier because I need to. He thinks I should continue to try and play tennis, that it would be good exercise for me and the baby. I want to lay around and sleep.

At the end of the day, no matter what happens or what we fight about, we always make up. It's a new rule we have for our relationship. No one leaves the house angry, no one goes to bed angry, and no matter how heated we get, we never say anything that we can't take back.

I found out the gender of the baby today. I didn't know that I was going to find out and I'm not sure that Ethan wants to know, but I know and it's driving me crazy. I want to tell him. I'm horrible at keeping secrets, and the thought that I have one is killing me.

I turn the lights down low, light the candles I put out, and sit down to wait. I have a card that I am sitting on. Inside is the sonogram photo the doctor gave me today. It's amazing how much these pictures have evolved over the years. The one I got today was three dimensional. Let's just say that I hope the baby does not look like the picture when it arrives.

I hear him pull in the driveway and immediately get nervous. He's going to know something is up the second he opens the door. I'm not very good at surprises. Having a candle-lit dinner with me is not the surprise.

I hear the garage door open into the kitchen. I hear him put his coat in the closet and drop his bag by the door. I know he's headed my way. I can feel him getting closer. The hair on the back of my neck reacts to his presence as he rounds the corner.

That smile. His dimple is winking at me, and it never fails to make me want to jump his bones. That's how we got in this predicament to begin with. He approaches with caution. I can't blame him. When he left for work this morning, I was angry. Not with him, not with anything in particular, just angry.

He kisses me on the top of the head and takes his seat across the table from me. Without saying anything, I fix him a plate and pass it over to him so that I can fix mine.

"So, is this your way of saying that you're sorry for being batty this morning?"

"I was not batty, I was emotional."

"You know, you won't be able to use that excuse after the baby comes."

"Hopefully, I won't be this emotional after that."

We eat in silence for a few minutes, both of us saying a silent prayer that I won't be this emotional after my pregnancy is over. I don't know how to breach the subject, and my leg won't stop twitching. I know that he's going to notice soon.

"So, how was your doctor's appointment today?"

Good. Now I don't need to bring it up. Thank you. Thank you. Thank you.

"It went good. Things are good."

"Just good?"

"Yes, things are good. I have to ask you something though. We haven't really talked about it, but did you want to find out the sex?"

"I figured we would. Why?"

"Well, the doctor gave me a sonogram and told me the sex today."

"Really? You know if we're having a boy or a girl."

"Yes."

"Well. Are we having a boy or a girl?"

I could hear the excitement in his voice. I was so glad to hear it, to know that he was just as excited about this as I was. But will he still be excited once I tell him?

"Yes."

"Yes what? Boy or girl?"

I reach under my leg and pull out the card that I've been hiding from him. I slide it across the table, and he immediately reaches for it and tears it open. I watch closely as it dawns on him what I'm saying.

"Twins?"

**Find out how Becca
& Ethan's romance ends…
through Ethan's eyes.**

Weakness

Holding On: Book Three
Ethan's Novella

Chapter One

"Hey man. What's up? I was just about ready to call you with my flight information." I zipped up my suitcase and stood it up next to the bed as I spoke. When he didn't answer right away I looked down at my phone to see if we had been disconnected. "Brad?"

"I'm here." I can hear the pain in his voice and immediately my thoughts go straight to Becca. What's happened to her? Something is obviously wrong.

"What's wrong? What's happened? Is Becca okay?" I'm talking a mile a minute and not giving him a chance to answer.

"Becca will be all right. She's a little shaken but she's physically fine. It's Natalie." You can hear the pain in his voice as the words slowly make their way to the surface.

"What's going on?" I'm scared to ask but I need to know.

"Becca found her passed out on the floor of her laundry room yesterday. They rushed her to the hospital because she was bleeding from her head and barely had a pulse. I met Becca at the hospital last night but Morgan told us to go home, get some rest and that he would keep us posted. Becca woke me up just before midnight after getting a text from Morgan saying that we needed to come back up there right away." I hear him take a deep breath. When he doesn't continue right away I have to start asking questions.

Weakness

"What else did he say? Why didn't anyone call me yesterday?" I'm angry. Of everything he just told me the one thing that stood out was that Becca woke him up which means that he slept over at her place. I know this should be the least of my concerns right now but it's all that stands out.

"It all happened so fast. I was planning on calling you this morning and letting you know what was going on. I figured if Morgan sent us home that she was going to be okay and that waking you up wasn't necessary." You can hear how sleep deprived he is.

"So…" I drag the word out, waiting for him to give me more information but he's mute. Something bigger is going on and I need to know. "What's the prognosis right now then?"

He clears his throat. "There about to take her into surgery right now. She has a brain tumor."

He's speaking so low that I almost didn't hear him but when his words finally register I feel like I've been punched in the stomach. It takes me a second but my brain finally kicks into gear. *Holy Crap!*

"I'm on my way. My plane takes off in a few hours so I will be there by morning. Can you still pick me up from the airport?" I'm pulling my suitcase towards the living room and searching for my keys at the same time. I have to get home. I was planning on coming home today anyway. Natalie told me to wait until after the package arrive to come home. It was there so now I was supposed to follow. That was our plan.

He hasn't answered me and it's almost as if I can hear the wheels turning. I take a deep breath and then another and he still hasn't said anything. I look down to make sure I didn't drop the call. He's still there. I'm about to ask him again if he'll pick me up when I hear him blow out a frustrated breath before finally speaking.

"No. I think you need to stay there for now. There's nothing you can do here. If Becca see's you now then all of our planning will be pointless. She needs to open that package. She needs to make the decision. If you show up here now… it will all have been pointless." I know that he's right but just the thought of Becca going through all of this alone angers me. I punch the wall next to me and instantly feel slightly better. "Take it easy man. Putting a few holes in your wall is not going to make you feel better right now. Let's wait to hear from the doctors after the surgery. I will call you back and if you still feel like you need to come home then I will make sure that you have a ride from the airport."

"Okay but I hope you realize that I don't plan on sitting around here forever. If she needs me then I will be there in a heartbeat."

"I know that and deep down I'm sure that she knows that. I have to let you go. I'll call you later and fill you in on what's going on."

"Okay. Thanks man. Give our girl a big huge for me." Did I just say "our girl"? *Crap!*

"Will do."

He disconnects our call and I fall down in the chair behind me. I let my head fall into my hands and close my eyes for just a few minutes. I need to get my head back on straight before I see her. We've been working on this plan for two month. I can't let my temper, or my emotions, blow it for me now.

Natalie told me that this would work. She said that all I had to do was to send the portraits that Becca purchased while she was here to her house and that she would set the wheels in motion. She was supposed to make sure that Becca opened them. She was supposed to make sure that Becca didn't emotionally break down.

None of that happened. That's probably why it's best that I stay here right now. Without that part of the plan happening first, everything after will have to happen differently. I need to come up with a backup plan, one that didn't include help from Natalie since it sounds like she's going to be in the hospital for a while.

I'm racking my brain, wondering what more I can do. I included a second portrait in the package, something I didn't even tell Natalie about. I took the picture when she was at the gallery and it captured every raw emotion she was feeling at the time. It was stunning. I was hoping that if she saw it she would realize how much she still loved me. If she doesn't open the package then I will never know.

I'm still racking my brain and willing my phone to ring hours later when it finally does and when Brad's number flashes across the screen my body goes on high alert.

"Hey man. I just talked to Morgan. I guess the surgery went well. He said that Becca is on her way home for a while. I'm going to meet her there to make sure she's gets some rest. We can't go in to see Natalie until she's awake."

"Alright well keep me posted. How is she?" I know the answer to my own question but I need to hear it from him.

"She's a mess but she's managing. Like I said, Morgan sent her home to rest. She's exhausted. As soon as I know more then I will give you a call." He's holding back something. You can hear it in his voice. I almost ask but my fear of knowing the answer keeps me from speaking.

I try to sleep but thoughts of Becca and Natalie keep my brain working in overdrive. It was after midnight here when I talked to Brad and now it's close to five and I still haven't fallen asleep. I give up. I crawl out of bed, start a pot of coffee and jump in the shower. I need to keep moving or else I was going to fall apart.

Goosebumps cover my arms and the hair on the back of my neck stands up only seconds before my phone starts ringing. I answer it without looking at the caller ID, knowing that whoever is calling me is calling with bad news.

The only thing that I heard was "coma". Nothing else sank in. I need to go home. I need to be there for my friends. I need to be there for Becca. Brad thinks I need to stay here, to give it more time. I know that he's probably right and that pisses me off even more.

I hang up on him before he can hear me put another hole in my wall. Why is this happening to us? Haven't we all been through enough? Natalie has been the glue that has been holding me together, holding Becca together, these last few months. She's shared her goodness with the world time and time again. She doesn't deserve this.

I sleep very little that night, if at all. I remember watching the hours tick by, thoughts of Natalie and Becca floating through my mind. I prayed for the first time in a long time. I prayed for Natalie to get better. I prayed for Becca to be able to hold it together without me by her side. I prayed that this wouldn't drive her back into Brad's arms even though I knew that right now that they were probably wrapped around each other. It was almost as if I could feel her soul crying.

I was surprised when my phone rang five very long days later and Natalie was on the other end of the line. I cried. The sound of her voice was such a huge relief for me that every emotion that I had been keeping bottled up was let loose the second she spoke.

We talked for only a few minutes but it made my heart lighter. She kept telling me over and over again that she was going to be fine. The more she said it the more I wanted to believe her but the less I did.

Natalie had never been very good at lying. She was either trying to convince me or herself. Either way, it wasn't working so I finally had to call her out.

"I'm glad you're feeling better but you need to realize that everything is not alright. Listen to yourself for a second. You're trying to convince yourself that you are going to be fine. What are the doctors saying?"

She was quiet for a second. I knew my words were somewhat harsh but no one else was about to call her out on her line of bull.

"They keep telling me that as long as I keep fighting that I have a chance. I won't let them talk to my parents or to Morgan anymore. They keep scaring the crap out of them." You can hear how angry she is. Good! Let her be angry. Maybe she'll use that anger to motivate her.

"That's because this is scary for all of us. None of us want to lose you."

"Well, I don't plan on going anywhere without a fight so you're not rid of me just yet."

"Don't say stuff like that. It's not funny." I'm yelling. I shouldn't be yelling but the way she said it... like it was no big deal. That just set me off.

"Listen Ethan. I need it to be funny. I need to keep my emotions in check and to keep things light. If I don't then I might fall apart and I can't do that right now. I need to be the strong one; for me, for Morgan, for everyone. If I don't put on a brave face then their pity will break me down and I don't know what I will do. This is so much bigger than what everyone thinks. So, it might not be funny but it's what's keeping me going right now. I know that in the end that I probably won't make it but for right now I need it to be funny so that I can keep fighting, so that I can keep a positive outlook. If you don't like it then you can hang up." You can hear the anger in her voice escalate. It's over powering all the other emotions that are trying to break through.

She called me every few days. You could hear the bitterness in her voice growing. She had started to sound less like the friend that I knew and had grown to love and more like the bitter person that I had expected the first time I talked to her. I was concerned, especially after she told me that she had started to push people away, but I also knew that I couldn't do much about it.

Her calls were like clockwork. My phone rang at the same time

Weakness

every three or four days. When she didn't call after five days I knew that she was taking a turn for the worse. She never wanted to talk about what was happening with her. We'd talk about things that weren't important. We'd reminisce about high school. We'd talk about our plan to get Becca and I back together. We never talked about her.

The day I realized that she hadn't called was the same day I got a letter from her in the mail. At first I just thought that it was odd that she was writing me a letter. Why? What is the point of writing someone a letter these days when you can just call them or email or even text? Letters are so old fashion.

That's what I was thinking before I read what she wrote.

Ethan,

I know that you're probably pretty surprised to be getting a hand written letter from me but there is a reason behind all of this. You and I have always been frank with each other and this letter is going to be no different. This is my good bye letter to you in a way.

I talked to the doctors yesterday and no matter what they say I know that I am not going to be able to beat this. If I'm wrong then great but, just in case, I'm writing letters to everyone who's important to me. I'm starting with you.

We've shared a lot of memories over the last few weeks and there was a reason for that. I needed to remember the good times because what lies ahead is not going to be easy. Not for me and not for anyone else. I need for you to help them all remember those good times.

I'm inclosing another letter in here that I need for you to deliver for me. It's important that you do this for me and since you can't really argue with me then I'm going to assume that you are agreeing to this. It's my eulogy. I need for you to stand up and read it to all of our friends and family. (Thanks)

As for our situation with you Becca... Here's my plan, because you know that I have to have at least a little bit of control of this situation. When the day comes, if the day comes, that I leave this place... Brad is going to call you and let you know. ONLY then are you allowed to get on a plane and come home. I know you are going to want to pack up right now and get on a plane and I'm asking you not to. Please.

Here's why... Becca is going to get a letter too and you know that she will need you there when she opens it. She'll need both of you. I have a feeling that she probably won't open it until either right before or right after the funeral. She won't have the strength to deal with it until then. She'll need you to help her find that strength.

You are her one and only, the one she is meant to be with for the rest of her life. She already knows this she just need to realize it and stop allowing herself to doubt everything. My letter will help but your presence will force her to make that decision. I'm pretty sure that at this point she hasn't opened your package. It's probably still sitting in my living room. That will help push her over the edge as well. Make sure she opens it.

This is it. Your chance to fix everything. As much as I had planned on being there to help you both I know that I won't be able to be. For that I'm sorry. I love you both so much. I need you to know that.

Please don't call me. I know are that you probably reaching for your phone right now and just the thought of talking to you, knowing that you've read this letter... well, I just can't stand that thought. It's too painful. So, put the phone down. Let this letter be the last conversation we have, as much as that sucks.

I love you Ethan. I always have in one way or another. What I love the most about you is the fact that when you love someone, you love then with your whole heart and nothing less. You give all of yourself to that person, heart and soul. That's the one thing we have always had in common. Make sure you never change that. Becca deserves all of you, the good and the bad.

Take care of my best friends.
Natalie

I clutched the letter in my hand for hours while I cried. I cried for Natalie. I cried for Becca and Morgan. I cried for Natalie's parents. I even cried for Brad. Most of all I cried for myself. I knew that I wouldn't see her again. I knew that I wouldn't talk to her again. I wouldn't have my opportunity to see her one last time, to say my good bye. I was going to respect her wishes and not call her and make this harder for her than it had to be. So I cried and let every emotion that I had been bottling up for the last six month out.

Printed in Great Britain
by Amazon.co.uk, Ltd.,
Marston Gate.